CAGED

DEFIANT KINGS
BOOK ONE

BELLA MATTHEWS

SENSITIVE CONTENT

This book contains sensitive content that could be triggering.
Please see my website for a full list.

WWW.AUTHORBELLAMATTHEWS.COM

COPYRIGHT

Copyright 2022
Bella Matthews

All rights reserved. No part of this publication may be reproduced or transmitted by any means, electronic, mechanical, photocopying, recording or otherwise, without the prior permission of the publisher, except in the case of brief quotation embodied in the critical reviews and certain other noncommercial uses permitted by copyright law.

Resemblance to actual persons, things, living or dead, locales or events is entirely coincidental. The author acknowledges the trademark status and trademark owners of various products referenced in this work of fiction, which have been used without permission. The publication/use of these trademarks is not authorized, associated with, or sponsored by the trademark owners.

This book contains mature themes and is only suitable for 18+ readers.

Editor: Dena Mastrogiovanni, Red Pen Editing
Cover Designer: Shannon Passmore, Shanoff Designs
Model: Chad Hurst

DEDICATION

To the little girl with big dreams.
Never stop going after them.
You're never too old.
It's never too late.

"Thinking of you keeps me awake.
　　Dreaming of you keeps me asleep.
　　Being with you keeps me alive."

— UNKNOWN

MADDIE

"Come on, Maddie... Ditch your class tonight. Grab a drink with me."

I look up from the floor, stretched out on my mat at the MMA gym where I teach yoga three nights a week, and smile at Hudson Kingston. The reigning world light heavyweight champion is the biggest flirt I've ever met, and he knows it. For the past two years, he's asked me out at least once a week. Of course, that number varies, depending on how many times he finds me stretched out on a mat.

Let's just say I've heard a lot of bad Downward Dog jokes since I started teaching here.

And since our mutual friends got married and moved in next to him, he's also managed to become a friend of mine too. But deep down, he'll always be a flirt at heart and refuses to let me forget it.

"You're in training, King. No alcohol for you." I stretch my legs out in a V and lay my chest flat against the mat, then raise my eyes to the man standing in front of my toes.

A slow, sexy grin extends across his chiseled face, and

warmth spreads through me. "Oh, I can think of a few other things we could do."

My friend's husband, Cooper, smacks the back of Hudson's gorgeous blond head.

Why do the gorgeous ones always have to be so cocky?

Because this man . . . this man is beyond gorgeous. He's six feet, five inches of rock-solid, golden muscles and beautiful black ink that's on display every single time he trains. They've just finished for the night, so he's changed into gray sweatpants and a dark-green Crucible hoodie that look almost as good on him as the low-slung shorts and bare chest do when he trains. But . . . but, but, but . . .

A deep chuckle rumbles from Cooper's chest. "You wouldn't even know what to do with a woman like Maddie, asshole. Can your dates even spell their own names?"

Hudson shoulders his gym bag and smiles his megawatt smile. Perfectly straight, white teeth that probably cost his parents a small fortune. "I don't give them an IQ test, Sinclair."

And there it is . . . there's the *but*.

Hudson Kingston is also a manwhore.

I have no doubt he could make my body sing. But as much as I'd give anything to let this man take the v-card I'd love to ditch if I could, I also have absolutely no doubt I'd get my heart crushed in the process. Which leaves me to settle for friendship with a side of the fun banter we've got going on instead. "You couldn't handle me, King."

This man was dubbed Hudson "The King" Kingston by the fighting world years ago.

On someone else, it might seem like an arrogant or self-indulgent name.

But it fits him like a golden glove.

"One night with me, and I bet I could have you loving how I *handle* all sorts of things, sunshine."

Our eyes lock for a single charged moment, but it's broken when the chimes above the gym door ring, and my students start shuffling in. *Saved by the bells.* I stand to greet a few of the girls from the local university and overhear Cooper telling Hud to get better lines.

But maybe he should just try using them on someone who's not broken.

"Thanks for coming." I hold the front door open as my students spill out into the parking lot. I honestly don't need to teach yoga anymore. I do it because I love it. And maybe because I'll always be a little paranoid about not having enough money in my savings account. My social-media management business has taken off over the past few years, but I still haven't entertained the idea of giving up teaching at Crucible . . . yet.

Waiting for everyone to filter through the door, I wave. "See you again next week."

Once the doors click shut, I lock them, then lean my head back against the glass and close my eyes for a hot minute. My soothing playlist for my favorite yoga class shuts off abruptly, and the gym's manager, Imogen, pops her head up from behind the front desk.

"Mads, can you close up tonight? I promised the band we could run through our new set, and I'm already late." She throws her crossbody bag on and grabs her keys from the desk. "Please, please, please," she pleads, and I shake my head no.

Sensing she's losing me, she adds, "I'll clean the mats for you for a week."

"Sold." I hold out my hand. "You should have started with

that offer." I hate cleaning the mats after class, and a week of not doing them sounds pretty good.

Imogen passes me the spray cleaner and spins her keys. "Thanks, Mads. I owe you one."

"Nope. You owe me a week." I take the bottle and singsong my response. "Have fun. Don't do anything I wouldn't do."

Imogen moves toward the door before swinging her red hair back around. "We're all doing things you wouldn't do, Mads. One of these days, you're gonna see what you're missing out on," she says on a laugh just before she disappears through the front doors.

My friends love to tease me about my lack of a love life. Like I'm single by my own choosing. Dating sucks in general. And when your brother is a pro football player who's more protective of you than anything in the world, it can get kinda . . . sticky. That, compounded with my own personal demons, and it's just not worth it sometimes. I go through phases where I try to put myself out there, but most of the time, I'd rather just be surrounded by my friends.

Life is easier that way. Less complicated.

A noise from the back of the building stops me as I spray down the mats. "Hello . . . ?" I call out, wondering if someone may still be in the bathroom.

Although, my students were all accounted for.

The gym should be empty.

Maybe something fell over.

An uneasy feeling washes over me as I look around the empty gym, then jump when the chimes over the front door sound.

It swings open a moment later, and Hudson walks through. "Mads . . . you still here? I forgot my phone." He scans the room, looking for me.

I raise my shaking hand to cover my pounding heart. "Oh my goodness, Hudson. You scared the heck out of me."

"Maddie," he hollers, his eyes growing wide as he spots me across the gym. Then he roars, "Move!"

I'm not sure what scares me more . . . the way his voice booms through the entire building or the look on his face as he charges me.

Instinctively, I move toward him. "Hudson—"

Out of the corner of my eye, I see movement behind me a split second too late.

Like the world has switched into slow motion and quicksand is holding my limbs hostage, I try to move, but fear freezes me in place.

Until Hudson knocks me out of the way with a rough shove backward.

I fall to the floor while my scream reverberates from the rafters.

There's a man in a black ski mask running from Hudson.

Oh my God.

Hudson catches up to the attacker easily.

The guy grabs a kettle bell and throws it behind him.

My scream gets caught in my throat when I watch Hudson jump over the black kettle bell. It's like a horror movie happening right in from of me, as Hud comes down and slips on the mat I'd just washed, landing on his knees.

The guy in the mask takes advantage of Hudson's misstep and moves like lightning through the hall and out the back door.

With my heart racing, I scramble to my feet and fly to Hudson's side.

Kneeling next to him, it's impossible to miss the pain etched on his face. "Oh my God. Are you okay?"

He reaches around me and cups the back of my head. "I'm fine, Mads." His eyes frantically search mine, and I think I'm seeing this tough MMA fighter petrified for the first time in the three years I've known him. "Are *you* okay?"

I nod, but the adrenaline begins to wane, and the world starts to spin.

I can't even begin to wrap my mind around what almost just happened.

Once he's satisfied I'm okay, he clenches his jaw. "Call the cops, Mads. Tell them to meet us at the hospital." He closes his eyes and tilts his head up to the ceiling. "I think I busted my knee."

With trembling hands, I make the call.

"HOW FUCKING LONG DOES it take to get the results of an MRI?" Hudson's older sister, Scarlet Kingston-St. James, hasn't stopped yelling since she and her husband, Cade, stepped into the private room Hudson was given as soon as we arrived at the hospital. Apparently, when a wing of the hospital is named after your family, they don't make you wait in the emergency room like everyone else.

Cade wraps his arm around Scarlet, attempting to soothe his wife, but by the looks of it, he's just fueling the fire. "He's going to be okay, duchess. They're both okay. It could have been worse."

Cade would know. He owns Crucible, and he's Hudson's coach.

My life has been intertwined with the Kingstons for years.

Despite that, I'm curled up on the chair next to the bed, feeling like an intruder.

There's nine of them, and they're the biggest, loudest family I've ever met.

It's all sorts of intimidating when you see it up close, even if it's the family dynamic I'd always wished for growing up. My brother, Brandon, is my only family. He and I grew up bouncing from one foster home to another. We've only ever had each other to depend on. So being around this crazy family has always been overwhelming.

Brandon plays professional football for the Philadelphia Kings—one of the teams the Kingston family owns—and I run the social-media accounts for a few of the Kings players, as well as the official account for the Philadelphia Revolution, the pro hockey team they bought a few years ago.

And I teach yoga at Crucible. At least I used to.

Please God, don't let him fire me for this.

But even as interconnected as we all are, I'm not part of this family. They're a tight-knit circle that I'm outside the periphery of. Watching but not part of. We share friends, and I've been to their weddings and championship games, but I've never felt like I belonged.

And I can't help but feel like I shouldn't be here for this.

While Cade and Scarlet continue their argument, which feels more like foreplay than him actually trying to calm her down, my eyes scan up Hudson's legs. They cut his sweatpants off at the knee, and he's been icing it on and off since we got here.

He reaches over with his big palm and squeezes my hand, sending a shiver dancing down my spine. "Hey, you doing okay?"

This man does not touch me . . . ever.

He flirts.

A lot.

But he never touches, and that's a good thing because I don't really like to be touched. And if this is what it feels like, I definitely need us to stay in a *touch-free* zone. Because for a hot minute, I consider what it would be like to crawl into that bed next to him and feel his arms wrap around me. And that's not something I do . . . ever.

"Mads," he prods.

"Yeah," I whisper. "I'm good. I'm just so sorry you got hurt. I swear I counted my students as they left, and the building should have been empty."

Scarlet spins around on her red-soled high heels. "Don't you dare apologize, Madison Dixon. This is not your fault." She looks at her phone for the millionth time tonight, probably checking to see if the news has gotten hold of the story yet. "Have you called your brother?"

Scarlet Kingston-St. James is a force of nature, and she's a hella scary one too. She runs the Philadelphia Kings, so she's Brandon's boss. Of course, this means she knows he treats me like a breakable piece of glass instead of a grown woman who owns a successful business and is capable of running her own life.

"Scarlet, back off." Hudson glares at his sister. "We're okay. You can reel in the momma-bear routine a bit, okay?"

She ignores him, keeping her sights set on me. "Madison, he'd want to know what happened."

"He'd want to fly home from London," I push back. The team just left for their first international game, and he's not due back for a few days.

Scarlet hands me her phone. "Call him. Tell him what happened, and do not let him fly home." This woman is used to getting her way. And normally, I'd envy her confidence and determination, but right now, I don't have the energy. I pull my phone from the pocket of my yoga pants and stand from the chair.

When I turn my head, I plaster a forced smile Hudson's way. "Want me to get you anything from the vending machine?"

Cade glares at me. "He's got two weeks left before his fight. No junk food, Mads."

"Sorry." I shrug my shoulders as Hudson drops his head back against the pillow. "I tried."

Just as I push through the door, Hudson calls out my name. "Mads..."

There's frustration lining his beautiful cobalt eyes when I turn around.

"Don't go far, okay?"

With a nod of my head, I step just outside the door and realize it wasn't frustration I was seeing in his eyes.

It was fear.

Hudson

"You've got to postpone the fight." Scarlet folds her arms across her chest and looks between Cade and me, like her word is gospel—written on a stone tablet.

I've been sitting in this goddamned bed for three fucking hours, and now, she's going to try lecturing me? I don't think so. I love my sister, but I'm pretty sure I earned a pass tonight. Let her husband deal with her.

Cade looks from the doctor to his wife, never even glancing my way. "He's hyperextended his MCL. It's not torn. He doesn't need surgery. He's a professional. We'll give him a few days' rest and have him training next week." The fucker finally looks at me with a cocky smile that's covering his concern. "Can you stay off your leg for a few days, King?"

"If it means I walk into that cage next week, you bet your fucking ass I can."

"I'll get the nurses to bring your release papers, Mr. Kingston." The doc heads out of the room, and my stomach drops. At least, this is manageable. It could have been worse.

It could have been a *torn* MCL or ACL, then it would have required surgery. Game over for months.

Scarlet moves next to the bed I'm still stuck in. "You're not going to let me talk you out of this, are you, Hudson?"

"Why ask the question when you already know the answer, Scarlet?" I crack my neck as the tension in the room grows. "I'll be fine."

"Sure you will." My sister tends to think she knows best. Especially when it comes to our family. She's not the oldest. That prize goes to Max. But in our family of nine, she's the oldest girl and has always been insanely protective of all of us. I'm used to that. What I'm not used to is the uneasy look in her eye as she glances Maddie's way again.

"Madison, did you speak with your brother?" Scarlet asks.

"He didn't answer, and I didn't think this was something I should leave in a text. He'd freak out." Maddie bites down on her bottom lip, probably uncomfortable having this conversation with Scarlet, and I have to shift on this stupid, fucking bed, so she doesn't see the insane reaction my body has every single time her teeth sink into her pouty pink lips.

Madison Dixon isn't the kind of girl you take out for a night, knowing it's only one night.

Everything about her screams she's more than that.

She's pure. She's sunshine.

Teasing her is fun. We flirt. We laugh.

But it never goes anywhere, even if my dick seriously wishes it would. I wouldn't have a clue how to give her what she needs. What she deserves. So, with a pain shooting through my knee, I shift anyway, needing to hide the semi I got from one look her way.

"I can't believe I'm going to suggest this," Cade groans and runs his palm down his face. "Mads, any chance you can stay with Hud for a few days? I know you work your social-media stuff from home, and I really don't trust the dipshit to stay in bed to rest that leg. Plus, I'm pretty sure your brother wouldn't want you staying at your house alone after what happened tonight."

Her head snaps up, and bright blue eyes practically glow with fire. "Seriously, Cade? Are you trying to say Hudson needs a babysitter? Or that I do?"

"Ohh . . . that's perfect. Does Daphne have a key to your house, Madison? I'll ask her to pack you some clothes and drop them off at Hudson's." Scarlet whips out her phone again, and I think Maddie might actually cry.

"Scarlet," I cut her off before she can steamroll Maddie. But apparently, my little ball of sunshine has a stronger backbone than I realized.

She doesn't stand or raise her voice. There're no arms crossing over her chest or stomping of her feet, something I've watched my sisters and best friend do over the years. She just holds Scarlet's stare, never looking away. "I can pack my own clothes, if I need them. But I haven't agreed to anything yet."

"Scar, can you give us a minute?" I ask.

My sister opens her mouth, but Cade interrupts her with an arm around her shoulders. "Come on, duchess. Let's go check on the kids." He guides her out of the room, giving me space to breathe for the first time all fucking night.

"You doing okay, Mads?" She's sitting in the same damn chair she's been in for hours. Her legs are tucked underneath her, and not an ounce of makeup is on her pretty face. Her long blonde hair is tucked behind her ear, emphasizing the fiery flush in her cheeks. She really is a ray of fucking sunshine. Always happy. Never curses. Sweet as can be. And she just stood up to Scarlet. I've seen grown men cower in front of my sister. I definitely wouldn't have thought Maddie had it in her.

"I really hate that the whole world knows my brother

treats me like a baby and feels like they need to do the same if he's not around. I'm twenty-four, Hudson, and your sister just talked to me like a teenager who needs to be told what she's doing until her daddy comes home."

"Maddie . . . First of all, if you've got a daddy kink, I'll be your daddy all day, every day."

She rolls her lips together, trying to hold back her smile, but eventually gives in to the urge. Her laughter breaks through the heavy weight of the room. "You're a moron. You know that, right?"

"I do. But Scarlet's not wrong. I'll need help for a few days. And maybe you shouldn't be alone until we know who broke into the gym tonight. He wasn't going for the cash box, Mads. He was behind you. It might be a win-win if you stay with me for a few days. You know . . . you scratch my back, I wash yours." Her smile is infectious when both dimples pop deeply in her cheeks, and something expands in my chest, knowing I made that happen.

Men have killed for lesser things.

"Come on, Maddie. You know you wanna."

"My goodness, Hudson. Did you take a class on awful lines or something? That was really bad." She rubs her hands over her bare arms, drawing my attention to the goosebumps covering her creamy skin.

I hadn't thought about the way we rushed out of the gym. It's freezing outside and only a few degrees warmer in this hospital room. Maddie's in a tank top and skintight yoga pants that stop just under her knees.

This woman gets cold in the heat of the summer.

I throw my hoodie her way. "Put that on."

"Excuse me?" she snaps.

"You're shivering." I watch as she shakes her head, mumbling something about men, but she does as she's told and throws my hoodie over her head. And it swallows her whole.

"Better?" she asks. I nod and ignore how much I *don't* hate seeing her in my clothes. "Do you even want me to stay with you?"

"Will you wear one of those little candy-striper uniforms?"

Scarlet picks that moment to walk back into the room. "She's not a stripper, dipshit."

"And you're two weeks out from the fight of your life," Cade chimes in. "No girls. No drama. No booze. The rules don't lessen because you're hurt, dumbass. They get stricter, and you know it. So, show me you can stay off the leg. If I don't think you can fight for even one second, I'm calling it off."

Maddie shakes her head like she can't believe what she's about to say, but her eyes stay locked on mine. "Fine. I'll stay with you and make sure you stay off your leg. But I'm doing it on one condition." She turns to my sister. "I do not want Brandon knowing what happened tonight until the team gets home Monday morning. I want him focused on the game, not arguing with me. You need your center focused."

Scarlet smiles a predatory smile. "Done."

"Three days, King. I don't want to see you at Crucible until Monday. You can work your arms at home. But don't even think about doing anything with your legs until Monday." Cade stares hard at me, waiting for my agreement, but I look over at Maddie instead.

"You sure, Mads?" The words trigger the internal battle I've had with myself for years. Maddie Dixon is my friend. And while it's been a bit of a struggle keeping her in that box, I've always done it because we're better off that way. But that doesn't mean I don't want more.

She's the only woman who's ever tempted me to want more.

To think about what that would look like.

To consider whether I'm capable of giving it to anyone.

The only woman.

Her being so damn close is going to complicate things. But the idea of her going home alone after that guy was so close to her tonight—what could have happened if I hadn't realized I left my phone at the gym . . . Yeah, she's not sleeping alone at her house tonight.

"It's fine. But the first time you put *Stepbrothers* on, I'm leaving." Her entire face brightens while everyone in the room laughs.

"It's a classic, Mads." I hold back my smile. "What do you have against laughing?"

"It's a dumb movie, Hud." She lifts her chin, doubling down on my favorite movie. "It's either me or *Stepbrothers*."

Like there's any fucking chance I wouldn't choose her.

MADDIE

"Sit down, Kingston. You're not walking up the damn stairs tonight." Cade and Hudson are arguing while I stand in the family room, staring out the wall of windows making up the entire side of his house. The snow has just started falling outside, and the view of the lake at the end of Hudson's backyard looks like part of a Norman Rockwell painting.

No matter how many times I see it, this view always takes my breath away.

Hudson's house sits on the banks of Kroydon Lake, and the waterfalls play a constant soothing melody in the distance. He moved in a year ago after spending months on renovations, and from the first time I stepped inside, I've been in awe of how warm and homey it is.

Not at all the bachelor pad most of us were expecting. Reclaimed wood floors and a stacked stone fireplace take center stage on the first floor, surrounded by windows and oversized, plush furniture. Everything about it screams beauty and comfort... and money.

Hudson spared no expense making this home his own personal retreat.

The Kingston family is Philadelphia royalty. They own half the city. It's easy to forget that when you're talking with them because they don't act like . . . well, like how I'd imagine billionaires would act.

Which I guess isn't exactly a fair assumption.

"Maddie . . ." I spin around to find Cade standing behind me. "He's on the couch, and he's grouchy. Don't let him convince you he's okay to walk up the steps tonight. Make him wait until tomorrow." He hesitates, then pulls his keys from his pockets. "You sure about staying here? You could always come stay with Scarlet and me until Dixon gets home."

"Umm, no thanks, Cade. My brother may like to think I need to be taken care of, but I did manage to live on my own for four years before I moved in with him. I'll be fine."

Cade laughs as he shakes his head. "I gotcha. But give him a break. We big brothers like to think it's our job to keep our little sisters safe. I think I was more upset when Imogen moved out than she was." He takes a step back and points toward the giant sectional sofa where Hudson's flipping through channels on the TV. "He's gonna be a pain in the ass, Mads. Call me if you need me."

"Okay. Thanks." I follow him to the door, then lock it once he's gone.

A chill runs down my spine, thinking about locking another door earlier tonight and what happened afterward. I pull the detective's card from my pocket and flip it over. I'm not sure what exactly he thought I'd remember and be able to tell him, but I was given instructions to call if anything came to mind.

I kick my Uggs off and sit them next to the front door, then pad barefoot over the cold hardwood floor into the

CAGED

kitchen in search of something to drink. The space is massive and open, with high ceilings and open shelving instead of cabinets lining the walls. Everything is spotless and sitting perfectly in its place, and I wonder whether that's because Hudson is secretly OCD or if he has a housekeeper.

My phone rings, drawing me from the rabbit hole my mind started spiraling down. When I pull it from my pocket, the face of my best friend, Daphne, is flashing back at me.

"Hey. I'm standing in your closet. What do you want me to pack for you?"

Daphne and I roomed together all four years in college. Then she lived with Brandon and me after we graduated. Of course, that was before she moved in with, and eventually married, Hudson's oldest brother, Max. "What the heck, D?" I lower my voice, not wanting it to carry into the other room. "What are you doing in my closet?"

"Scarlet called and asked me to pack you a bag. What the hell happened?"

I grab two bottles of water from the fridge and look to see if Hudson has any wine hiding in there. It's going to be a long night. "I'm fine. Someone broke into Crucible tonight. Hudson tried to catch them but slipped. He hurt his knee, but he's going to be fine too." *I hope.* "Scarlet's making too big of a deal out of this. I can get my own clothes, D."

"You sure you know what you're doing, Mads?"

"What do you mean? It's only a few nights. I'll be fine." I pull myself up to sit on the granite counter. "He's not hurt too bad. He can put weight on it, but it's swollen and sore. I should be fine to help for a few days."

I hear Daphne going through my closet and unzipping a bag, then she groans, "That's not what I'm talking about, and you know it. You two have danced around each other for years."

"Hudson flirts with everyone, D. We're friends. That's it. I think I can resist him for a few more days." It's not like I have much of a choice. "What do you think I'm going to do? Jump into bed with him?" Heat prickles my skin again, and I can't believe how hot that idea makes me.

"He's not a long-term guy, Mads. And you're not a one-night-stand girl."

"I guess stranger things have happened. I mean, look at you and Max." I laugh quietly as I look around again. I definitely didn't see myself ending up here tonight. "I'll be fine, D. I'll call you tomorrow."

"I guess so. Just be careful. Love you, Mads."

"Love you too, D." I end the call, grab a banana from the counter, and hop down. Then I pull out a pack of peas from the freezer and snag the towel sitting next to the sink before I hurry across the cold floor to where Hudson sits reclined on one of those fancy armchairs at the end of the sectional. His leg is raised in front of him, and a commentator on ESPN is discussing his upcoming fight.

Hudson looks up at me, and the look on his face breaks my heart a little. "How are you feeling, Mads?" There's no silly smile, only exhaustion pulling at the corners of his eyes.

"You're the one who got hurt. Because you were making sure I was safe." Once the towel is wrapped around the peas, I place them gently on his knee. "The doctor said you need to keep ice on it."

Hudson pats the couch next to him. "Sit down, Madison. You look like you're about to fall over."

"I'm fine." I hold up the banana and water. "Are you hungry?"

He takes them from me and puts them on the end table. "No. I ate before I came back to the gym. How about you? Have you eaten anything? Do you need to test your sugar or something?"

I stare at him, not sure why I'm surprised he'd even think

to ask that. Everyone knows I'm a diabetic, even if it's not something I make a big deal about. "I had some trail mix at the hospital. But I should probably check my sugar. And maybe take a shower. I never got one after my class tonight."

"The shower in my bathroom is the only one with soap and shampoo. It's at the end of the hall at the top of the stairs." He points behind me. "There's a linen cabinet inside with clean towels and a laundry basket by my bed that has clean clothes in it, if you want to borrow something."

"Thanks. I'll take you up on that. Daphne's going to drop my stuff off later tonight. Do you need anything?" I ask, trying to push down my discomfort at the idea of invading Hudson's personal space.

He flashes me a forced grin. "Nah, sunshine. I'm good."

I grab my purse and quickly make my way up the stairs and down the long hall. The door to his bedroom is open, but when I step into his space, it feels wrong.

There's something intrinsically intimate about being in this man's room.

An unnerving level of comfort that makes me squirm.

Another fireplace sits in the corner of the room with two chairs off to the side and a huge bed anchoring the space. The furniture looks well-loved, not brand new. And it dawns on me that this isn't a space meant to be seen. This is a private space he's comfortable in. And I'm not sure if *I'm* comfortable being in here.

I like flirty Hudson. He's easy to spar with.

He's easy to disregard as a serious threat to my heart.

This . . . this is something else.

Something about this makes it just a little harder to keep Hudson Kingston in the box I've put him in. A flashy and ostentatious bedroom would have firmed up my manwhore assumptions. It would have helped me strengthen my walls. This . . . for some reason, this may have created the first crack in those walls, that I've solidly fortified since I was a little girl.

Hudson

Maddie slips up the stairs, and I grab my phone from the end table. The damn thing hasn't stopped vibrating since we left the hospital. No doubt, my family's message thread has been blowing up. That's never a good sign.

My brothers, sisters, and I are definitely codependent.

We're loud. We're obnoxious. And we're viciously loyal to each other.

We can always count on each other to have our backs. You can also always count on them to serve you your ass when you fuck up. And when I look at the screen and see my sister Lenny yelling at me, I wish I could say I'm surprised.

> LENNY
> Hudson Thaddeus Kingston. Are you insane?
>
> BECKET
> Legally speaking?
>
> JACE
> Ohhh. She middle-named you, Dude. That's never a good thing.
>
> SCARLET
> I didn't tell you so you could yell at him, Eleanor.
>
> SAWYER
> Tell her what? What does Lenny know that I don't?

CAGED

LENNY

The total tonnage of things I know that you don't is immeasurable, big brother.

BECKET

Fair point, Len. But one thing at a time. What's going on with Hudson?

LENNY

Someone broke into Crucible tonight while Maddie was there alone. They think Maddie was the target. Hudson stopped him.

SCARLET

Technically, he fell. Then the guy ran away.

MAX

He saved Maddie. That's a good thing, Len.

JACE

Daphne's hot friend Maddie? The yoga teacher with the great ass?

MAX

Don't beat your meat to images of my wife's friends, Jace.

SAWYER

Yeah, jackoff. Don't beat your meat? Who the fuck says that kind of shit, Maximus?

AMELIA

Is Maddie okay?

SCARLET

She's fine. She's staying with Hudson for a few days to make sure he stays off his leg.

BECKET

Are they canceling the fight?

HUDSON

No. We're. Not.

SAWYER

You okay, brother?

HUDSON

I'm fine. Maddie's fine. The gym is fine. Now everyone can fuck off for the night and stop blowing up my phone. I'm going to bed.

JACE

With the hot blonde?

BECKET

There are other ways to get women, Hud. You don't have to hurt yourself to get their attention. Although asking her to kiss your boo-boo could work.

HUDSON

Fuck off Becks.

JACE

Seriously. Have you seen her when she teaches that yoga class? She makes downward dog look really good.

AMELIA

Jace, you're supposed to be the cute one. Not the pig.

SCARLET

Jesus Christ.

LENNY

Stop. Just stop. Where did we fail you?

HUDSON

Do you have a death wish, little brother?

JACE

Like you're not all thinking the same thing.

ONCE I CLOSE out of the group text and take the peas off my knee, I try to settle my mind without any luck.

I'm defending my title in nine days.

Nine fucking days, and I'm supposed to stay off my leg for three of them.

I'm in good shape.

Hell, I'm in *great* shape. But I still have fifteen pounds I need to cut before the fight. And every minute of training matters when you're in that ring. Cocky is great for show, and the league loves a good show. But cockiness doesn't win fights. Hard fucking work does. And being laid up for a few days is going to blow.

There's a knock at the front door before it swings open, which means one of my siblings just walked in. Some days, I regret giving them keys, but it's something we've always all done.

My brother Max, and his wife, Daphne, walk into the family room with a suitcase, book bag, computer bag, and a cat carrier in hand.

Damn. Women need a ton of shit.

Daphne opens the metal gate on the carrier, and Maddie's black-and-white cat, Cinder, darts across the room. The damn thing hates me. I haven't been around it much, but it hisses and swishes its tail whenever I've been at her house.

"Where is she?" Daphne asks with a hand on her very pregnant belly.

"Taking a shower." I motion toward the staircase, and Max and I watch his wife take the book bag up to Maddie.

Max looks me over before his eyes settle on my knee. "How are you feeling?"

"Sore as shit. But I'll be fine." I adjust the peas and wince. "I'm assuming Scarlet called."

Max nods. "How's she doing? What the fuck happened?"

"She seems okay. I don't know if it's hit her yet. That guy

was behind her. He wasn't going for the money or for Cade's office. He was behind her. I've never been so fucking glad to forget my phone in my life."

"Have the police said anything about any leads yet?"

"Not yet. But I'm going to call them tomorrow."

"Pretty sure Scarlet's already given them hell," Max huffs before he motions toward the TV. "Turn it up."

They're interviewing Spider Ramirez. This fuckhead has wanted my title for two goddamned years. He hasn't earned the fight, but that hasn't stopped him from talking shit about me and Crucible every chance he's gotten.

Asshole.

Max leans against the back of the couch. "You gonna give in and fight this little shit after you win next week?"

"Fuck him. He's gotta earn it."

I put in my time. He's gotta do the same.

Even with a bum knee, I'm not worried about winning next week's fight.

You don't train like I do year-fucking-round and have a doubt.

My thoughts stop on a dime when the sweet scent of honey and vanilla wafts into the room. *Her* skin always smells like honey and vanilla. Even after she's finished sweating through a hot yoga class, Madison Dixon smells delicious.

And like a man searching for an oasis in the desert, she draws me in. I want to taste her skin. Her lips. Her fucking cunt to see if she's as sweet as she smells.

It takes a few more minutes before she finally walks back into the room and takes my breath away. She drops down on the couch and lets Cinder curl around her. "Hey, baby," she purrs at the damn cat, and that voice... fuck me.

When she stands up with the black and white furball in

her arms, Daphne hugs her and whispers something that makes Maddie blush.

Max grips my shoulder. "I think that's my cue. Call me if you need anything."

"Thanks, man."

Maddie walks my brother and sister-in-law to the door and locks it behind them, then joins me on the couch.

Close, but not touching.

Because Maddie never touches.

Not unless I initiate it.

There's a story there.

One I've never asked about. But I will . . . eventually.

Her flawless skin has a warm pink glow from her shower, and her long hair is damp and hanging down her back. An old Philly Kings t-shirt is slipping off one bare shoulder and hangs down to her knees, covering the top half of her bare legs, and fuck me . . . she's got a pair of socks that look like they're made from a sweater pulled up to her knees. I've got no clue why that's so sexy. But my new goal in life might be to fuck her with those socks on.

Goddamn, I'm an asshole.

She's fucking perfect, and I'm fucking screwed.

I run my hand over my face and remind myself of Cade's rules.

No drama.

No booze.

No women.

Two more weeks of camp before the fight.

"So," she hesitates and tucks her legs up underneath herself. "Do you get the Hallmark channel here, King?"

Fuck me. It's going to be a long night.

MADDIE

Hudson has four bedrooms upstairs, besides the master. I walked by each one on my way to the shower, so I knew they were there before I got comfortable on the couch last night. I also knew I should have excused myself and gone to bed in one of them when my eyes got heavy after the first half of *Harry Potter and The Sorcerer's Stone*. Apparently, Hudson gets every channel *except* the Hallmark channel. But *Harry Potter* is my favorite movie franchise, so I ignored my body begging me for a bed and my brain telling me I should probably have sat on the opposite end of the sectional, far away from the ridiculously sexy man I was here to help. Luckily, even I knew that was ridiculous, and I convinced myself to stay right where I was. I could go to bed after Harry, Hermione, and Ron saved the day.

Only I never made it to that scene.

The last thing I remember was Hudson tugging a big cream blanket from the back of the couch and forcing me to share the softest blanket I'd ever snuggled under with him. I thought about saying no. I considered going to bed, like a coward with her tail between her legs. Then Cinder curled up between the two of us and surprised me when she rubbed up against the man who causes butterflies to take flight in my belly.

He ran his hand down her back, and to my complete surprise, she let him.

Traitor.

I was jealous of the cat.

Friend, Madison. He's a friend. That mantra played over and over in my mind while I overanalyzed the space between us. It wasn't like I was staying in the family room. He was planning on sleeping on the couch . . . I wasn't.

What do they say about the best laid plans?

Stupid plans.

Those beautiful windows I loved yesterday really suck when the sun shines blindingly through them first thing in the morning. Definitely more effective than any alarm clock I've ever set. But once the light wakes me up, it only takes seconds to realize where I slept last night. Because right now, my head isn't resting on a soft pillow. Nope. It's resting on a hard body.

I scrunch my eyes closed tightly, not ready to face the humiliation of admitting that not only did I fall asleep, but I also managed to rest my freaking face against Hudson's thigh.

I peak quickly through my lids, then slam them shut again.

Yup. Right next to his . . . *Ohmygod* . . .

Hudson is completely reclined, sleeping on his back with his arms tucked behind his head, and I'm practically molesting him with my face inches from his dick. *Inches.*

I never even sleep through the night. Daphne used to tease me about it in college. I'm a ridiculously light sleeper. Constantly moving while growing up did that to me. Always sharing a room with new people. Never trusting anyone. I hear everything.

How . . .? *How* . . .? How did I let this happen?

"You're thinking really hard down there, Mads. Stop. It's too early for that shit." Humiliation burns my skin while Hudson's raspy, sleepy voice puts a halt to my spiraling thoughts. He shifts beneath me, and I thank God I'm at least not lying on his hurt leg, as his big palm runs over my hair and down my back.

Amazingly, I resist the urge to jerk away and instead push up slowly, like I'm not a psychopath who hates to be touched. Because for some reason, I don't *hate* it when he does it. His warm palm settles on my back, and I sit up. "Sorry. I meant to go to bed last night. I can't believe . . ."

"Maddie, relax." Hudson's dark eyes soften as they search my face. "It's not a big deal." Yeah, to him I guess it wouldn't be. This man has probably slept with more women than I'll know in a lifetime.

"Of course." I shake off that horrific thought and the stabby urges that come with it and stand, only to be stopped when Hudson grabs my hand. My eyes snap to his fingers against my skin, and he drops it immediately.

"I was just gonna say thank you for your help last night."

"No problem." At least none I'm going to tell him about. "Are you hungry? I can make you breakfast." I know the words spilling from my lips are rushed and shaky, but there's nothing I can do to control them.

"Nah. I'm good. Just a little sore."

I tug the blanket from his body to look at his knee, but instead my eyes lock on the impressive bulge tenting his sweats. Holy . . . *wow*.

I force my eyes back to his knee. The swelling is down from last night. "Let me get you some peas, so you can ice your knee before you start moving around." I can only

CAGED

imagine what kind of lunatic I look like when I bolt from the room.

I hate this.

I'm not this person.

I don't get nervous like this.

Not anymore.

And I really don't like that I'm doing it now.

Pull it together, Madison.

I'm stronger than this. He's just a man, like any other man. But that's the problem. Hudson Kingston isn't like anyone I've ever met. Maybe this wasn't such a good idea after all.

Ten minutes later, Hudson has another bag of peas on his knee and a protein shake in his hand.

"Hey, Hud?" I ask as I walk back into the family room. His head tips back, and it really isn't fair how good this man looks first thing in the morning. I just looked at myself in the bathroom mirror and cringed—full-on cringed. And he looks like he's ready for a photoshoot or something. Totally unfair.

"Where'd you go there, sunshine?"

Good question. How about to a place I'm never going to tell him about. "What's your Wi-Fi password? I've gotta get some work done today."

The front door slams against the wall behind it, setting off the alarm as Imogen storms in. Hudson grabs his phone to turn off the obnoxious beeping, then watches the fiery red ball of anger that's his best friend as she storms into the room.

"Hudson Kingston. Why did I not know you stopped a goddamned burglar last night and got hurt doing it? And why the hell didn't you call me when you needed help?" Imogen might be yelling, but I know her well enough to recognize the hurt in her voice. These two are tighter than most siblings I know, and she's not even one of his sisters.

She stands in front of him, her arms folded over her chest, glaring at him, and fortunately, ignoring me.

I grab my bag from the floor where Max left it last night, and wave when Hudson looks over at me and mouths *help*. "Sorry, dude. You're on your own."

Imogen never takes her eyes off her best friend. "Are you okay, Mads? Cade said you were fine."

"Good as gold, Gen. Just going upstairs to get dressed." I hold in my laughter when Hudson grimaces, like he's bracing for more yelling, and slip upstairs. I know better than to get in between those two when they fight.

Instead, I'm grateful for the reprieve while I pull myself together.

It's going to be a long week.

Hudson

Once Maddie goes upstairs, I pull myself up from the couch and stretch out my sore muscles. My knee is throbbing in tune to my fucking heartbeat already. Great sign for how the day's gonna go.

I hobble into the kitchen on the crutches the hospital sent home with me, tuning out Imogen, who's still grumbling behind me. I should have already run five miles around the damn lake this morning instead of sleeping on the couch with my leg in the fucking air.

Who the fuck can sleep like that?

Not me, that's for sure.

On top of the ridiculous position, it's hard to fall asleep with a beautiful woman next you. Her sweet scent invading my senses didn't help me any. And that was before she fell asleep with her head tucked against my shoulder. Before she managed to slide down until her face was using my quad as a damn pillow. Inches from my dick. Sighing those sweet little sighs. Sounds I want to hear while my tongue is buried in her pussy.

Fucking hell. This woman.

I don't do this. I don't obsess over women.

Especially during training camp.

They're a distraction.

And I learned a long fucking time ago that distractions are dangerous.

She's my friend. Like Imogen . . . *but not*. Imogen has always been like a sister. From the day I met her, she was like Scarlet, Lenny, and Amelia. I'd do anything for her, but I've never fantasized about seeing her naked. Something I may or may not have imagined about Maddie more times than I'd ever admit while spanking it in the shower.

"What's wrong with you?"

When I turn around, Imogen's standing in the kitchen, looking at me like I've lost my shit. She might not be far off. "What's wrong?" I shake my head. "It's less than two weeks out from the biggest fight of my life, and I can't put weight on my left leg without pain. I can't train. Fuck. I couldn't even make it upstairs to get a goddamned shower last night. I slept like shit. I'm in pain, and I'm tired. Does that about sum it up?"

"Hud . . . why didn't you call me? I would have come over." She sits down on a stool at the island and waits.

"I don't know, Gen. It happened fast, and I was just thinking about whether I was going to be able to fight next week. The hospital took forever. Scarlet yelled at everyone. Cade was trying to keep her calm, and Maddie barely said a word. It just kind of happened. They suggested she stay here for a few days, and I went with it. I didn't really want her going home alone, if I'm honest." I move across from her and lean my weight against the counter. "The guy was right behind her when I walked in. Too fucking close. I don't know . . . It scared me. And we both know I don't get scared."

Imogen's bright green eyes stare at me, assessing. "Uh-huh. This has nothing to do with the crush you've had on Maddie Dixon since she started working at the gym then?"

"Seriously? A crush? What are we . . . thirteen? I don't have a crush." And even if I did, now wouldn't be the damn time to talk about it . . . Or act on it.

The fight's in eight days.

Nothing else matters until then.

She taps her fingers against the counter and cocks her head to the side. "Okay. I'll drop it—"

"Good," I interrupt her, but Imogen keeps talking.

"If you can tell me you don't have feelings for Maddie."

"I'm eight days out from this fight, Gen. It doesn't matter if I have feelings for Maddie right now. It's not going to matter the day after the fight either, because Maddie's looking for Mr. Forever. We all know it. And I'm not that guy."

Imogen picks up an apple from the fruit bowl and throws it at my head, then groans when I let go of the crutch and catch it. "Don't talk about yourself that way, dumbass. Just because you've never been that guy doesn't mean that you can't be. You just need to find someone worth it, and you know it."

I glare at her and take a bite of the apple.

I'm not sure what I'm supposed to say to that.

My dad fell in love more times in his lifetime than the average person ever will. And he cheated on all his wives. All but one. Lenny and Jace's mom was the real love of his life, and if he cheated on her, he never got caught. Not the best example of relationships to live with growing up.

The only thing it showed me was what I didn't want to do.

The kind of husband I never wanted to be.

"Hey, Gen . . ." I tap her foot with my crutch, needing to lighten the mood. "Want to help me in the shower?" I wiggle my brows, just before her elbow jabs me again.

"Eww. No." She pushes me away. "Call one of your brothers. Hell, call *my* brother. I don't want to see your junk."

Turns out, I don't need to call Cade because he calls me ten fucking minutes after Imogen leaves to make sure I'm staying off my leg. He also tells me he talked to the cops, and they don't have any leads. It looks like a random break-in. "Thanks, man. I'm taking it easy now. Tomorrow, I'll stretch and see how it feels."

"Take it easy. Start slow. You're in great shape, man. You've done the work. You're not one of those guys who gets fat and lazy between fights. You've got this. You're gonna be fine." The busy gym hums in the background. The metal clang of weights hitting the floor. The beat of the music blasting through the speakers. The dull sound of voices. They're all the sounds of home.

Crucible is my favorite place to be.

It's ironic that inside that cage is where I feel alive.

And for the first time since I bought this house, I fucking hate that I'm stuck here.

MADDIE

"I thought Daphne was exaggerating when she told me how codependent the Kingston siblings are." She'd just married Hud's oldest brother, Max, and couldn't get over how often they all stop by each other's houses or how much time they spent texting each other. "I was wrong."

Carys Sinclair closes her mouth and tries to hide her laughter over my rant. She's used to them by now. We've been friends for years. And lucky for me, she and her husband, Cooper, live next door to Hudson.

Hud and Cooper are currently in the home gym, doing whatever Hud's allowed to do for now, with strict instructions from Cade and the physical therapist at the gym to not put weight or stress on his leg. Meanwhile, Carys and I sit on the couch in front of a fire, working on the social-media presence for the holiday push for her company, Le Désir. She designs the most beautiful lingerie I've ever seen. I've splurged on a ton of it, even if no one has ever seen me in it.

It's dinner time on a Friday, and I'm still working.

I guess that could be one of my issues.

You'd think Hudson's siblings would be busy running

their freaking empire because King Corp definitely falls into the empire category. But no . . . Not these people. "Becket and Lenny swung by at lunch to check in," I continue my rant, deciding I'm fired up and not even close to done yet. "And . . . I may have also overheard a conversation earlier between Hudson and Sawyer. And I know that there's been a group text happening because he's either grumbled over it or laughed about it all day. All day, Carys. All freaking day. How do they get anything done?"

She peers over the top of my MacBook, trying hard not to laugh at me. "Mads, you and Daphne look at this differently than I do. I come from a big family. This is what we do. I'm used to it. We may not be as . . . *involved* in each other's lives as the Kingstons, but my family chat blows up on a daily basis."

"Says the woman who married her stepbrother." I can't help but tease her.

"Best move she ever made too." Cooper walks into the room and drops a kiss on top of his wife's head. "Right, baby?"

She rolls her eyes before tilting her head back to kiss him.

And that's when I melt.

That . . . That's what I want.

That easy kind of love.

The kind you work your butt off to get, then bask in for the rest of your life.

"Whatever you say." She sighs, then sips her wine. "Where's Hudson?"

Coop takes the glass from her for a sip, then hands it back. "He's on the phone. Sawyer called."

"Told you," I laugh as the man in question shuffles gingerly into the room, grumbling, with his crutches tucked under his arms. I don't miss the tension holding his body hostage before he sits on the arm of the couch next to me.

He tugs a strand of my hair until I turn around to face him. "What did you tell them, sunshine? Are you giving away all my secrets?"

"I don't know any of your secrets." Even if I wish I did.

And damn him for that.

"Carys . . ." Hudson turns his attention her way. "Sawyer just told me Six Day War is doing a surprise set at Kingdom tomorrow night." He lifts his brow. "Happen to know anything about that?"

Her smile grows a mile wide. "I wasn't allowed to say anything until they were sure they were coming." Six Day War is one of the biggest bands in the country right now, and Carys knows them well.

She lived with them and sang with them back when she was in college.

The lead singer's sister manages the band and is one of Carys's best friends.

They're also my favorite band.

I squeal like a lunatic and look between Carys, Cooper, and Hudson. "Oh my God. Please say we're all going Saturday. I've been dying for them to come to Philly again."

"Since my brother owns the bar they're playing at, I'm pretty sure I can get us in, sunshine." Hudson's being sarcastic, but I don't care because I want to see them again so badly. They played at Cooper and Carys's wedding last year, and to see them in that small venue was all it took to make me a fan for life.

The doorbell rings, and Cooper steps out of the room to grab what's hopefully our dinner and not another Kingston sibling. "Do you think you'll be okay to go to the bar this weekend?"

"You worried about me, Maddie?" His words are a step above a whisper, which does crazy things to my body.

I stare into the depths of his cobalt eyes, lost for a second.

Of course, I'm worried about him. He's my friend. Even if this feels like more.

Carys stands with her empty wine glass and clears her throat. "More like she's worried Cade will kick her ass if you screw up your leg any worse, Hud." She holds her glass up to me. "You sure you don't want any?"

I shake my head and wait for her to go into the kitchen, so it's just Hudson and me still in the room. "How are you feeling? You guys were in the gym for a while. You're supposed to be taking it easy."

"It's sore, but I've had worse. I took it easy, and we just worked arms. The damn stairs were worse than the workout." He reaches toward me, like he's going to touch my face, but I pull away. Hudson drops his hand, and the look in his eyes turns glacial. "Don't worry about me, Maddie. But we're going to talk about *that* one of these days."

I blink, shocked by the tone in his voice just as Cooper announces, "Dinner's here."

"There's nothing to talk about, Hudson," I murmur as I get up, ready to hurry from the room before he can push harder.

And thank goodness, he doesn't push.

Just waits for me to walk in front of him, then follows me into the kitchen.

"Hey, Carys . . ." She spins around to face me. "Want to pour me a glass of wine too?"

"Oh damn." Carys looks between Hudson and me, silently questioning the uncomfortable look on my face. Then she settles on him. "What did you do?"

Hudson drops down onto a chair at the kitchen table and props his leg up on a second one across from him. His knee is still swollen and bruised, so I grab the peas again and lay them over his knee, refusing to make eye contact.

"I didn't do anything," he answers her while he watches me.

Cooper hands Hudson his to-go container of grilled chicken and steamed vegetables and laughs. "Sure, you didn't. When they say they're not mad . . . that's when you know you're really in trouble."

I level Cooper with a glare as he passes my salad to me.

"I'm not mad, Coop." My voice comes out sharper than I intend, and he laughs at me.

Ugh. They all suck.

Hudson

My little sunshine spent the rest of the night pissed.

Not loud and yelling like any of my sisters would have done. No. This woman got quiet, and that was somehow worse. I watched it happen. She didn't shut down, not in an obvious way. And she covered it well.

Maddie still smiled and laughed when she needed to over dinner, but that smile was forced, and her words were quiet. She was making herself smaller, and I fucking hated it. Almost as much as knowing something, at some point in her life, caused her to pull away from being touched.

Not by everyone though.

Carys hugged her goodbye, and Maddie embraced her with no problem.

But that look in her eyes earlier . . . Even if it was just for a split second, I saw it.

And I wanted to fucking eviscerate whoever put it there.

Then I realized *I* put it there.

"Maddie."

She finishes drying the wine glasses, then turns around, but doesn't make eye contact. "Listen, Hud. I'm exhausted, and I need to sleep in a bed tonight. Do you have any preference which room I take?" She dries her hands and carefully hangs the towel back up, busying herself.

"Madison. Stop." The words come out sharper than I intend, and I cringe at her reaction.

She wraps her arms around herself and continues to look anywhere but at me. "Let's not do this, Hud."

"Maddie . . ."

Finally, she lifts her pretty eyes to mine. Her golden hair frames her face like a halo. "Please . . . Can we just *not?*"

I stand very fucking carefully from the table and grab my crutches, knowing I overdid it today and I'm paying the price tonight. *Fuck*. Slowly, I move across the kitchen and lean back against the counter next to her, taking care not to touch her but positioning myself barely an inch away. "Why don't you like when I touch you, Madison? Is it me? Are you scared of me? Do you think I'm going to hurt you?"

She closes her eyes, and damnit, I think she's gonna cry.

But that's not Maddie.

This tiny woman is stronger than that.

She steps in front of me, with her eyes locked on my chest. Then with a shaky exhale, she flattens her palms over the cotton of my shirt against my pecs.

I suck in a sharp breath, my hands aching to wrap around her. To hold her. To comfort her. To soak in just a little bit of her light and warmth, but I don't. This is her show now, and she needs to be in control of it.

This is the first time in three years this woman has ever willingly initiated any kind of physical contact with me. And the jolt of electricity it sends coursing through my veins is better than any adrenaline high I've ever gotten.

Finally, she lifts those long lashes and gives me her eyes. "It's not you, Hudson. I know you'd never hurt me. I swear to God, I know it. It's just . . ." She runs her teeth over her bottom lip, composing herself, then traces the ink that's visible above my shirt.

"You've touched me over the years, Hudson. Maybe not as much as you've touched everyone else, but you've still done it. If I was scared of you, you'd have known it, and you would have stopped."

"I've always wanted to touch you, Maddie." The words slip out quietly, and there's so much truth behind them. Not the smartest thing to say. Not the smoothest or most practiced. But it's the honest truth.

Maddie drops her hands and takes a step back, breaking our connection. "You shouldn't, Hud. I'm broken." Another step takes her further away, and I miss the connection immediately. "Do you care which room I sleep in?"

I shake my head because words fail me for the first time since my dad died.

"Good night, Hudson." She walks away, leaving me alone with my thoughts.

"Night, sunshine."

MADDIE

Does counting the rotations of the fan count as meditation?

Because it's sure not helping me calm down.

I've been up here for an hour, and there's no way I'm falling asleep any time soon. Not with my emotions riding a roller coaster like it's a weekend at the Jersey shore. I've always loved the roller coasters.

The bigger, the faster, the crazier, the better.

I love that feeling of your stomach dropping as you fly around the loops backward, not able to see what's coming at you. I always thought they were an adrenaline high and would beg Brandon to ride them again and again.

I wish I was fearless like that in my real life.

I wish I could take what I want and not worry what was coming at me.

Not worry about the consequences.

Not let the past determine my future.

Knowing there's no chance I'm falling asleep anytime soon, I shoot a text to Daphne.

> MADDIE
> Any chance you're awake?

> DAPHNE
> Yeah. What's up?

I HIT Daphne's number and watch her face appear in her dark bedroom after one ring. "What's wrong?"

"Nothing . . ." She gives me the look—the one only your best friend can give you because words aren't even needed. "I don't know, D. Everything?" I'm not even sure why I called her, but I need to figure this out.

"You made it one whole night, huh?" She gets up and tells her husband she'll be back. "What did he do?"

Daphne knows me better than anyone in the world, and I love her for it. She was the first person I ever let in who wasn't Brandon. I trust her with my life, and because of her, I've got a tribe of women who surround me and support me. But it took a long time for me to feel that level of comfort. And I don't know if I'm capable of giving anyone else that same kind of trust.

Because I'm broken.

"He didn't do anything, D. It's me. You know Hudson. He's a touchy-feely kind of guy, and—"

She cuts me off, "And you're not a touchy kind of girl."

"Exactly." I hesitate, before adding, "But what if I want to be?"

Daphne sits down on her couch and wraps a blanket around her shoulders. "Do you?" My heart squeezes at the hesitancy in her voice, like I'm a deer caught in headlights she's expecting to bolt. "I'm going to ask you something, Mads, and I don't want you to get mad at me."

"I won't get mad, D."

"Do you just want to be touched, or do you want Hudson to touch you? There's a big difference between the two, and I want you to really think about the answer."

I sit up in bed, bringing my knees up to my chest and wrap an arm around them, really considering her question. Thinking about the way my body warms under *his* hands. How it warms, just imagining what it could be like. He's the only man who's ever made me feel that way, and I'm not sure what to do with this realization. "I think I want Hudson . . . It's not that I want anyone else to touch me. Just him."

"You think or you know?" Daphne pushes.

"I'm torn, D. I know what I want, but I don't know if Hudson's capable of giving it to me. And I don't know that it's fair to ask him if I'm not sure what I'm doing." I close my eyes and try to picture what that conversation would look like, but I can't. "It's the first time I've ever wanted it. Truly wanted more. All the dates I've gone on . . . All the guys we met in college . . . Not one of them ever made me feel the way I felt tonight with my hands on his chest."

"It's a nice chest," she sighs. "And we'll circle back to the fact that your hands were on it later."

"It is a very nice chest," I laugh softly, breaking the heavy weight hanging in the air. "I'm sorry. Did I wake you up?"

"Nope. This kid has been kicking hard tonight. And when she's not practicing her soccer skills on my kidneys, the heartburn is making sure I can't lie down anyway." She angles the phone down so I can see her big, pregnant belly.

"I still can't believe you're going to be a mommy."

"Me either." She brings the screen back up to her face. "Mads . . . I can't believe I'm about to say this about Hudson Kingston, but he's Max's brother, and I love him, so I'm saying it anyway."

I wait for a long beat, wondering what words of wisdom she's going to lay at my feet.

"Don't hurt him, Maddie. He might seem invincible, but he's not. He's a really good guy, with a really big heart. Be sure of what you want before you make any decisions. Because from what I've seen, when the Kingstons fall, they fall hard. They love hard. And if you give him your heart, I don't see how he could ever let it go. Because you, Mads, are incredible."

My emotion at her words gets caught in my throat. "I doubt we have to worry about me hurting Hud, D."

"Just keep it in mind, okay?"

"I will." I would never want to hurt Hudson or Daphne. "Love you, D."

"Love you too, Mads."

A creak in the hall a few minutes later has me watching a shadow that stops on the other side of the closed door. My heart races, wondering if Hudson's going to knock. But after a minute, the shadow is gone, and the footsteps head further down the hall to the next room. Hudson's bedroom.

I sit there, paralyzed and debating what to do for at least ten minutes as disappointment chokes me. Until I finally get up, positive this is insane but forcing myself to move until I'm standing in front of his closed door with my hand pressed against it.

"Maddie?" he calls from inside the room.

"Yeah," I whisper back.

He doesn't say anything, but the door opens, and I swallow my tongue.

Steam is billowing in from the master bathroom, *and wow . . .*

This man is beautiful. Standing with one crutch under his arm, a towel wrapped around his hips, and his wet hair dripping down his face, I'm not sure I've ever seen anything sexier. I rake my eyes over all the beautiful, inked muscles on display and have to fight the sudden urge to reach out and trace every last line.

It's a new urge, and I don't hate it.

"Are you okay, Mads?" He adjusts his hold on the crutch, still favoring his sore knee and searching my face for an answer. "Maddie?"

I take a deep breath to settle my thoughts as they go into overdrive. "I'm fine. I just . . . God, why is it so hard?"

Hudson cocks his eyebrow, and I realize what I said. More importantly, what it sounded like. "Not you, you big goof."

"I know, sunshine. I just wanted to see you smile. You never smiled tonight. Not your real smile anyway." Hudson steps back. "Let me throw some pants on."

"Okay."

He moves into the walk-in closet, nearly out of view but not completely.

No . . . I can't tear my eyes away, as the black towel hits the plush carpet, and am rewarded with an unobstructed view of one calf before it's covered by a pair of dark jersey pajama pants. When he steps back into the room, he's shirtless with just those pajama bottoms hanging from incredibly lean hips. Of course, this king has those damn dips that form a perfect V leading to . . . trouble. *Yup.* I bring my eyes back up to meet his and see a devilish spark staring back at me. *Definitely leading to trouble.*

Hudson ambles across the room and presses a button that closes the drapes, then sits on the bed with the TV remote in his hand. "Come on, Mads. I want to see what happens in the next *Harry Potter*. Watch it with me."

And like a moth to a flame, I throw caution to the wind and walk into the room.

Oh. My. God.

Ohmygod . . . Noooo.

I know, without a doubt, exactly where I am the next morning before I crack open a single eye. Wide-awake Maddie might hate the idea of being touched, but apparently, I turn into a little ho when I'm sleeping and can't get enough of it. I hold myself still, unsure if I'm trying to soak this moment in before I have to get up or if I'm scared it's a dream I don't want to end. Hudson's arms are wrapped around me, and so is that clean, crisp scent I swear makes me stupid every time I'm near him.

There's an incredibly hard body beneath me.

And this time, it's not just beneath my face.

No. Because that wasn't humiliating enough.

It's beneath a leg, half my chest, an arm, and my face.

I don't move a muscle while I listen to Hudson's even breathing and say a quick prayer to every god I've ever read about, and some I may have only heard of in some less than stellar books, that if I move off him slowly and carefully, he won't wake up. Because seriously . . . if I'm going to do the walk of shame for the very first freaking time, I should have at least gotten an orgasm I didn't give myself out of it. Not just a *Harry Potter* movie.

I don't think I've ever moved this slowly in my entire life, but somehow, I manage to extricate myself from Hudson's bed, without the man in question waking up, and basically run back to the other room to get dressed and get out of the house.

Once I'm in my car, I send him a text, grab a protein bar from my purse, and head to my house. It doesn't take me long to get there, but figuring out what the heck I want to wear tonight is a whole different story. I want to look . . . hot? Sexy? I don't know what I want to look like. I just know I'm not finding it in this closet, so after close to an hour of indecision, I call in the reserves. *Figuratively speaking.*

MADDIE

Who's going to Kingdom to see Six Day War tonight? And what are we wearing?

CARYS

Well, you already know I'm in. I've got a strappy silk top and a little leather skirt I was thinking about wearing with knee-high boots.

CHLOE

I'll be there, but I've got no clue what I'm wearing.

CARYS

Yes she does. Doc Martens and skinny jeans. When was the last time you wore anything else?

CHLOE

Whatever. Fine. Yes. My purple Docs, black skinny jeans, and a sheer white shirt with a beautiful black bra we just added to the line.

DAPHNE

You all suck so bad. Max doesn't want to go. With the baby due soon, he'd wrap me in bubble wrap if I let him.

MADDIE

That's sweet.

DAPHNE

More like overbearing. But his dick is huge, and I'm horny all the time, so he has his purpose.

CHLOE

Sounds like a good problem to have, D.

DAPHNE

Mads - Are you at your house or Hudson's?

MADDIE

Mine. You didn't exactly pack me concert clothes. LOL

CARYS

Ohh. I've got a great dress we just designed that would look incredible on you, Mads.

CHLOE

YASSS. The navy blue one?

CARYS

Yup.

CHLOE

I've got the shoes.

MADDIE

Guess I'm coming to your house, Carys.

DAPHNE

Good thing you live next to her then.

MADDIE

I don't live there. I'm staying there for two more nights. BIG difference.

CHLOE

And what room are you sleeping in Mads?

MADDIE

...

CHLOE

I will totally take one for the team and report back on whether he's worth giving that cherry to, Mads.

MADDIE

The hell you will.

CHLOE

OMG. I got Maddie to curse!

CARYS

And why shouldn't she? You're not interested, right?

MADDIE

You guys seriously suck.

DAPHNE

No we don't.

MADDIE

Yes you do. You said so earlier.

DAPHNE

I was right when I said it. You're being a baby. Woman up, Mads.

CARYS

Yup. Pull those big girl panties up. But make sure they're pretty lace ones. And let Hudson take them off with his teeth.

CHLOE

Or rip them off with his bare hands.

CARYS

That's really expensive lace, Chloe.

CHLOE

Have you seen Hudson Kingston? I'd let him rip anything he wanted.

And that's when I turn my phone off . . .

Is it possible to love your friends and hate them at the same time?

Hudson

Okay, so calling last night a long night is the understatement of the century.

Maybe the fucking millennia.

Maddie and I didn't talk about what happened earlier in the kitchen. I didn't tell her that every protective instinct in my body was demanding that I wrap my arms around her and promise her no one would ever hurt her again. Because I have no doubt she was hurt, and when I find out by who, I will hunt them down and kill them myself.

Once I dangled *Harry Potter* in front of her, it only took her a moment to decide watching it in my room didn't need to be any different than watching it downstairs.

She was wrong.

We both were.

She climbed into my bed, and we both sat there, leaning against the headboard with the blanket pulled up over us to watch the movie.

I may have needed to cover her bare legs because they were wreaking fucking havoc on my sanity. And that shit was already dangling by a very thin thread. Having her in my space . . . in my bed, where fantasies of her spread out beneath me played out in my mind like a home movie. *Yeah*. I needed to cover both of us up before she started to think I was a horny asshole.

Not that she'd be wrong about that.

I don't know why this woman likes these damn movies, since she can't stay awake till the end to save her life. And this one wasn't even as good as the first one. It was a little over halfway through when her head rested on my shoulder. I waited until the end of the movie to move so we were both lying down. I probably should have woken her up so she could sleep in her own room, but I liked having her in my bed with me. I was a gentleman about it, though, and kept a few inches between us. Even if I didn't want to. Even if every bone in my body was screaming for me not to.

Madison Dixon crawled under my skin years ago, and I've ignored it. She's my friend. It's better for her that way. *It's better for both of us that way.* That's what I've told myself. But I've always known there was something about her. Every time I'd hear her talking about another date gone wrong—and there have been a ton of fucked up dates—I always felt relief.

That's not how a friend should feel. I should want her to find someone. To be happy.

I shouldn't want to tell her none of those guys are good enough.

And I definitely don't need to tell her I am—because I'm not.

These last few days have made those less than platonic feelings really hard to ignore.

Curled up on her side with her hands under her face, she looked like a damn angel, and something primal in me liked having her in my bed. Like it was where she belonged, even if there was no way I'd be able to sleep. I figured I'd be awake all night because my dick was hard and I refused to do anything about it. But it turned out that wasn't the only reason. Madison Dixon is a bed hog. She's also a goddamn ice cube. Her feet could flash freeze whatever they touch . . . and they touched me. A lot. And they're not the only thing that touched me. Nooo . . . She's a cuddler.

It started with her cold feet being shoved between my legs after she'd managed to inch her way across the bed. My eyes popped open, thinking some kind of fucking cold-ass poltergeist was under the sheets with us. But within minutes of warming up her feet between my legs, she rolled her entire body against me, fully twined her legs with mine, and threw her arm across my chest. Then she sort of shimmied against me until she got comfortable, sighed the prettiest sigh I've ever fucking heard, and never moved again. Not once. All. Night. Long.

And when did I start categorizing a woman's sighs? Seriously? What the actual fuck?

Here's the thing . . . within seconds, she'd warmed up. From the tips of her ice-cube toes to the top of her sexy smelling head, she warmed up and lay lax against me while I stared at the ceiling, trying to figure out what the hell I was supposed to do with my arms. Maddie was obviously asleep. My little sunshine spent half the night pissed because she doesn't like to be touched. And fucking consent can't be given if she's asleep.

So with my hands folded behind my head, I spent most of the night staring at the ceiling, telling my ragingly hard dick to take a fucking break because the soft, now entirely warm woman who had wrapped herself around me was not going to do anything more than sleep tonight.

Tonight being the keyword . . . Because I swear to God, this woman is getting to me in ways no one ever has. And I'm starting to think there's a reason for it, and I'm an idiot for ignoring it.

Lenny and Jace's mom used to say everything happens for a reason, even if you don't know what that reason is while it's happening.

Is there a reason we're being pushed together?

I still don't know if I can give her what she deserves, even if it might actually be what I also want.

And when she woke up this morning and snuck out of bed like her ass was on fire, I let her think I was sleeping because what the fuck am I supposed to say to her? I don't think, *Hey Mads, I think we should explore this thing between us, but it's gotta wait until after the fight*, is gonna work.

She ran outta the front door pretty quickly after she left

my room, and my phone pinged with an incoming text after she left.

> MADDIE
>
> Hey. I ran to my house to find something to wear tonight. Didn't want to wake you. Let me know if you need me to pick anything up while I'm out.

Oh, sunshine. That's how we're gonna play this?

HUDSON

"Mads . . . If you actually want to see the band perform tonight, we've got to go," I yell from the bottom of the steps.

"I'll be down in a minute." Yeah . . . sure she will.

I check my phone again and see another warning from Cade. He's pissed.

I worked with the physical therapist from Crucible this afternoon, and it felt good. He said I'm fine to get back into the gym on Monday, and that I can ditch the crutches now. But he wants me taking it easy tonight and tomorrow.

Cade wasn't thrilled that my version of taking it easy was a night at Kingdom.

Oh, ye of little faith.

Like I'm an asshole kid who's gonna get drunk, get in a fight, and snort a line of coke off a hooker's tits or something. I've got more discipline on any given night than most people will ever hope to have. Does that mean that I miss out on some of the fun?

So. Fucking. What.

It's what I need to do to get what I want.

And what I want is to be the best this sport has ever seen.

If it means I go to bed at the same damn time every night, eat bland chicken and steamed vegetables every day, and treat my body like the temple it is, bring it on. If not, I wouldn't be here with multiple championship titles already behind me.

One week away from my next one.

Hell, at this rate, it might not even matter because I'm not sure we're actually making it to the bar tonight. Maddie's been getting ready for over an hour.

I wouldn't even be going if it weren't for her.

But she seemed so damn excited about seeing the band, and for some reason the idea of her going without me left a nasty taste in my mouth.

I grab my keys from the table in the hall, then turn when I hear heels tapping against the hardwood stairs.

"*Damn*," I breathe out, surprised I've got any breath left.

Maddie's freckles dance against the pretty pink flush that moves up her cheeks. "Is that a good *damn*?" she asks, before she spins in a circle, showing off her dress from all angles.

And not a single angle disappoints. It's a dark-blue, silky thing that kind of clings to her body without being skintight. It dips down in the front, showcasing a mouthwatering tease of her chest, with a bit of extra fabric that's held together by tiny straps tied around her neck and trailing down her bare back.

There's no way she's wearing a bra, and I don't see even a hint of a panty line on her barely covered ass.

Ho-ly. Fuck. She's trying to kill me.

"It's an excellent *damn*, Mads." I clear my throat and grab my coat from the back of a chair. "Where's your coat?"

She places her phone inside a small purse and closes it with a smile. "No coat."

"It's twenty-two degrees outside, Madison." I stare at her, waiting for her to grab something, but she doesn't move.

"I don't have one here, Hudson. I only have a sweatshirt, and I'm not wearing that. I'll be fine. Plus, I'm pretty sure we won't be waiting outside in a line at your brother's bar." She takes a few steps toward the front door, then looks over her shoulder and bats her lashes. "Are you coming?"

It's pretty fucking hard to think straight when every last ounce of blood has left my brain and gone to my dick, so I silently drape my peacoat over her shoulders as we walk to the car.

Once I open her door, she sits down in the seat and crosses her legs. That damn dress barely covers her ass and rides all the way up her thigh, causing my brain to short-circuit. "Thanks, Hud."

I raise my eyes to hers and fight unbelievably hard to not stare at her firm nipples pressing against the silk of her dress.

Fuck me. That's one fight I'm happy to lose.

WHEN SAWYER BOUGHT Kingdom a few years ago, he threw everything he had into it. We all knew it would be a success, but none of us had any idea *how successful* it would become. The converted old warehouse takes up an entire block of cobblestone streets in Old City, Philadelphia.

There's a line wrapped around the building on any given night, full of people waiting to get inside to hear a band, have a drink, and enjoy the cool industrial vibe happening. Luckily for us, he's also got a VIP section, complete with restricted access and a private bar sitting at the top of a black metal staircase, overlooking the dance floor and stage below.

That's where we're hanging tonight. Becket and I have claimed the corner table, while Cooper dances with the girls downstairs. Max is home with his very pregnant wife, and Jace is approaching us now, late, as usual. The only thing that little shit's ever on time for is hockey practice.

"Hey, bitch-ass. How are you feeling?" He drops down into an empty seat and grabs Becks's beer.

Becks gives him a *What the fuck?* look. "Bitch-ass? That's the best you can do? You're a hockey player, brother. Shouldn't your smack-talk be better than that? You better up your game before you go pro."

I glare at our youngest brother. "Who you calling bitch-ass, you little spanker? Even hurt, I can still take you."

Jace lifts his arm to show off his muscles, then smiles. "You wish you had guns like these."

"Jesus Christ. You gonna whip your dick out next, asshole?" Sawyer stands behind him, then passes out another round of beer. "Put that shit away before Hudson sends you back to school, crying to your coach."

Sawyer has been coming and going as he deals with whatever the hell he's dealing with downstairs. The place is a madhouse since word leaked that Six Day War was doing a surprise set tonight. Imogen's band, Sinners & Saints, did their normal set earlier, and the crowd's getting anxious, waiting for the main event. "Where's your girl, Becks?"

"Shh," Jace groans. "Don't ask about the dragon queen."

"Don't insult the dragons." Sawyer drops down into the seat next to me, then laughs when Becks flips him off.

Becket has been with his girl longer than any of us thought it would last, and not a single one of us can figure out why.

"What's caught your eye, Hud?" Sawyer watches me closely, then looks over the open railing of the VIP section—down to the dance floor below as the band talks to everyone between songs—then settles back in his chair. "Oh, I've got you. It's not a what, but a who."

There's no way to miss who has my attention.

Maddie stands dead-center in front of the stage, with a light shining above her, giving her a golden glow. Cooper, Carys, and Chloe are all there with her as they cheer on the band.

But damn . . . It's her. She's fucking incredible.

"How are things going with Maddie?" Becks asks, happy to have the attention off him for a minute.

"Yeah, Hud. How *are* things going with the little yoga teacher?" Jace lifts his beer to his lips with a fucking smirk I want to knock right off his face.

"Shut the fuck up, jackoff. She's got a name, and nothing's going on."

Jace raises his hands in fake surrender. "Hey, you just seem upset for a guy who's not interested in the girl. So you wouldn't care if I go down and dance with her for a while, right?"

He stands before Becks shoves the chair into the back of Jace's knees, knocking him forward. "Knock it off, kid. Don't be a dick."

Jace ignores Becks and pushes back, then flips him off. "I'm getting another beer. Anybody need anything?"

Nobody does, and we all watch him cross the space to the bar before Becks turns back to Sawyer and me. "That's his third beer. What's going on with him? He hasn't been here that long. Does he seem like he's in a shit mood to you?"

I shrug. "Leave him alone. It's the end of the semester. He's probably got finals happening, and I know he and Max have been arguing about him entering the draft."

"I swear to God, I'm never having kids." Becks squirms.

Sawyer and I both laugh.

"Both of you can fuck off."

Sawyer stands back up. "Listen, I've gotta get back downstairs, but I meant to tell you Spider Reynolds is downstairs with his entourage."

"The guy with the serious hard-on for you? I saw him talking shit on the sports channel the other day," Becks adds.

"Yeah. We all have. The dick wants a fight, but he hasn't fucking earned it. I don't give them away. You wanna fight me—get in line and pay your dues." We might all have to fight each other in the cage, but most of us shake hands afterward. There's a respect there for the sport and for each other. But this douche has neither.

Sawyer looks down at the stage then back at me. "Yeah well, it looks like he's made his way to your girl."

That gets my attention. I push up from the table and look down at Maddie. Sure as shit, this asshole has managed to move himself next to Coop and the girls.

Fuck this.

Maddie

Chloe and I scream as Jack Madden, Six Day War's lead guitarist and Carys's former roommate, pulls her up on stage to perform a song she helped write, while Cooper looks on with pride beaming in his eyes.

"She's incredible," I tell him as Carys lights up the stage.

Cooper never takes his eyes off his wife. "She really is."

Chloe grabs my hand and pulls me toward her to dance when we're jostled by a group of guys next to us. "Oh my gosh . . . sorry," I tell them as she spins me into the group.

A gorgeous man with dark hair and darker eyes catches me with a big hand on my hip and a predatory smile on his face. I back away automatically, and his grin grows. "Now, where're you going, pretty girl? The fun's just getting started."

Cooper moves between us and them protectively. "Sorry, guys. No fun tonight. They're with me." The group of men close ranks as Cooper moves us behind him.

The guy I bumped into straightens to his full height, and I see him differently.

He may be tall and handsome, but he's got a presence I know well.

It's hard to miss a fighter when you're surrounded by them all the time. And this guy reeks of it. "How about you let the ladies speak for themselves? They seemed to be having a good time until you got involved." The stranger attempts to move around Coop but stops when a familiar hand pulls me back.

Hudson moves in next to Cooper, attempting to block my view as the crowd surrounding us begins to take notice of what's happening, not that I'm even sure of what's going on.

"Back the fuck up, Spider." Hudson's hands ball into fists at his sides, and my own fight-or-flight instinct kicks in. This man cannot get into a fight tonight. He can't . . . He can't get hurt. He can't get in trouble. He can't give them any reason to take away his title fight next week.

With my heart about to beat out of my chest, I move around Hud and place myself between him and whoever this guy is.

I place my hand on Hudson's pecs and look up at him. His eyes flare with rage. Only now, it's directed at *me*. "Move, Madison."

He doesn't lift his hands to me.

Always respecting my boundaries.

But he's pissed. And I'm the new target.

"Listen to your bitch, King. She knows you're not so big outside the cage. Knows you can't beat me. I mean, I can see why you'd let her have your balls with an ass like that."

My head whips around in time to see this disgusting man

take a step forward, and his eyes look me over from head to toe. "When you're ready to ride a real man, you come see Spider, baby. I'll show you what you're missing."

Hudson takes a step forward, and I grab his hand and pull him away.

Completely aware that he's letting me do this.

"Maybe I should start calling her to get you to fight me, King. Is that it? That how I can finally get that title? Looks like she's the one calling the shots. You go have your fight next week. Beat another chump. Like it's hard."

Hud stops, and everyone around us takes a step back, feeling the anger radiating from this normally controlled man. "I'll fight you anywhere." He takes a step closer. "Anytime. Anyplace. But I don't fight for free. You've got to earn it. Now fuck off and get the hell outta my brother's bar." It's like the entire dance floor has decided to completely ignore the world-famous band on the stage and watch these two fighters instead.

When he turns back to me, his fingers lace with mine, and I don't dare pull away. An eerie calmness covers the unchecked fury in his dark-blue eyes. "Come on," are the only two words uttered before Becket meets us at the door with Hudson's coat and my purse in his hands.

"You okay?" Becks looks between the two of us, and I'm not sure if he's asking me or Hud.

Hudson opens the bar door and guides me through it before answering his brother through clenched teeth. "I'm good. We're leaving."

He drapes his coat over my shoulders while we stand silently, waiting for the valet to come back with the car. "Hudson—"

"Don't," he cuts me off. "Not right now, Madison."

Eventually, he holds my door open, then rounds the front of the car and gets behind the wheel.

The twenty-minute drive back to his house feels more like twenty hours.

He never looks at me. Never speaks to me. Nothing. Not a single word. And I hate every minute of it, but I have no idea what *I* did or if he's even mad at me.

By the time we pull into his garage, I want to scream, and that kind of outburst goes against every instinct I've ever had.

Once Hudson turns the car off, I decide to take my chances and turn toward him. "I'm—"

"Nope." He opens the door and gets out of the car. "We're not doing this yet." Then he slams the door behind him, and I watch as he stomps up the stairs and goes inside.

What?

Is he kidding me?

I follow him into the house, my own anger growing as I try to decide whether he's mad at me or just mad.

And there he is, leaning against the counter in the kitchen with his head hanging low.

"Hudson—"

His head snaps up, and those dark eyes hold me hostage. "Don't, Madison. Don't speak. Not yet. You have no fucking clue what you did tonight."

I tentatively step into him, forcing his head up and ask quietly, "What I did? Explain to me what I did. Because as far as I can see, the only thing I did was remove the two of us from the situation."

Hudson swiftly picks me up and deposits me on the counter, so we're eye level with each other, then cages me in. "What you did was put yourself in the mouth of the goddamned lion, Madison. You put yourself between two trained fighters instead of trusting me to handle it. Trusting me to protect you. That's my world. Not yours."

I press my palm flat against his chest, not pushing him

but instead giving myself space to breathe. "I didn't want you to get hurt again because of me."

"You don't get it. I wouldn't have gotten hurt. But you could have. And there's no fucking way I don't kill that guy if he accidentally hits you instead of me. You've seen me fight, Maddie. But that's been controlled. There are rules in the cage. Rules we all follow. There aren't rules in a street fight. And I'm not gonna be controlled if something happens to you." His hand slaps the counter next to my thigh, and I shiver. Not in fear . . . but at the way his skin grazes mine.

"You can't put yourself in danger for me. That's not how this works. You need to trust that I'll always keep you safe." Hudson lifts his hand to cradle my face, and a chill races down my spine. "I can handle getting hurt. I can't handle *you* getting hurt."

"Hudson . . ." I fist his shirt as I search his eyes for an answer to my unasked question.

I hate that I put him in this position.

I hate that he's mad at me.

And I really hate how desperate I am for him to kiss me right now. "I'm sorry. I . . . I didn't think."

A wave of emotion sweeps over his face before he drops his hands and steps back. "No. You didn't." Without another word, he turns on his heels and walks out of the kitchen and up the stairs, leaving me speechless and wondering what the heck just happened.

Eventually, I head upstairs and stare at the clothes in my suitcase.

I was supposed to stay the night and go home tomorrow, but I don't stay places I'm not wanted. Not anymore. Not ever again. And Hudson is fine. If he could go out tonight, he doesn't need me here. I honestly think he didn't need me at all, he just didn't want me alone after the break-in, and that simultaneously aggravates me and melts my anger a little.

I've never been confused by this man in all the years I've known him.

We're friends. That's it. I'll always wonder if there could be more between us, but it won't work. It can't. And I can't do this to myself. I refuse to.

With my mind made up, I throw on a pair of leggings and a hoodie, then grab my stuff from the bathroom and toss it into my bag. I didn't have that much with me, so it only takes a minute to pack it up before I'm adding my MacBook to my work bag and sitting it on top of my suitcase, ready to go.

When I turn around, a scream gets caught in my throat.

Hudson stands in the doorway, staring at me. He's changed into his sweats and a white t-shirt that's stretched across his chest. A tight look lines his eyes. He's definitely still mad.

"You're leaving?" he asks. Only he doesn't sound mad, so much as hurt.

I mirror his stance. "I'm not going to stay where I'm obviously not wanted."

He moves into the room and slides his hands up my arms.

I don't pull away. I can't. And after a moment, I realize I don't want to.

Not when we're this close. Not tonight.

He lifts his head to the ceiling before bringing his eyes back to mine, but a different kind of fire is sparking in them now. "I've wanted you every single day since you walked into Crucible three years ago, Madison."

"Oh," is all I manage to squeak out in shock before I pull it together and tip my head back to look at him. "But you were mad."

"Yeah. I was. I still am. Because the idea of you getting

hurt makes me see red, Maddie. But that doesn't mean I want you to leave. It just meant I needed a fucking minute to pull my shit together and stop seeing red." He wraps his arms around me and rests his chin on the top of my head, holding me there until I finally soften and lay my face against him. "I'm sorry I made you feel like you weren't wanted. Don't leave."

"I'm sorry too. I didn't think about any of the ways my getting in the way could go badly. I didn't think past making sure you didn't get hurt." Giving in, I finally wrap my arms around his waist and surrender to the feeling of being in his embrace.

I'm not sure how long we stand there in silence, but somewhere along the line, I let go of my anger and breathe him in.

He presses a kiss to the top of my head. "Come on. You said the third *Harry Potter* movie was your favorite." He tugs me behind him into his room, and the two of us crawl under his covers before he pulls the movie up on his TV.

"Mads . . ." he says over the intro music I know by heart.
"Yeah?"
"I'll never let anything happen to you." The sheer honesty in his voice adds another crack to my walls, and I move closer to him and rest my head tentatively on his shoulder.

"I know that," I whisper quietly.

Neither of us say another word as the movie plays. And I guess, unsurprisingly to either of us, I spend another night in his bed. Sleeping soundly. Completely safe.

HUDSON

She was going to leave.
Why does that feel like a sucker punch to my gut?

Maddie managed to stay awake for all of the third *Harry Potter* movie but fell asleep only a few minutes into the fourth one. She climbed into my bed, and unlike last night, she didn't leave any space between us. And after only a few minutes, her head rested on my shoulder, but she was awake this time.

I guess our moment in the kitchen changed something.

Because when Maddie's hands reached out for me . . . when she grabbed my shirt, whether she realized it or not, she pulled me toward her. She wasn't trying to prove a point. She wasn't convincing herself she could touch me without flinching or pulling away. There was a connection, and she needed it as much as I did.

The want in her eyes didn't escape me.

It was there, pulsing between us. Need recognizing need.

But I'm not an asshole, even if I like the world to think I am.

I'd never take advantage of her, and that's what it would have been.

Taking. Especially in that moment, when she was vulnerable.

So I walked away. I knew I needed time to get my shit together before I did something neither of us was ready for. Not yet. Not after tonight. Not with the fight a week away. I need to focus, and I'm pretty sure my little ball of sunshine is going to need some time to figure things out on her own. She doesn't like to be pushed. I already know that.

But seeing her packed up and ready to leave didn't work for me.

This right here . . . her in my arms. This is what I needed, and judging by how quickly she relaxes against me, so did she.

Whether she realizes it or not.

Something about this is different than it was last night. I give it a few minutes after she falls asleep before I turn the TV off and roll us both over. With my arms wrapped around her, she snuggles in like that's exactly where she's meant to be, wiggles her perfect little ass right up against my dick, and sighs.

I swear to God, her fucking sighs do me in.

We're spooning. *Fucking spooning*. Maddie might be the inexperienced one, but I wonder what she'd think if she knew I've never done this before. Any of this. I don't sleep with women. We fuck. They leave. Occasionally, I leave. It's the only way it works.

Women have always wanted something from me.

More than I'm willing to give.

Maybe they want to say they've slept with a fighter or a champion.

Or they want to take their shot with a Kingston.

Those women don't even care which Kingston, they just

want our name and what comes with it. But not Maddie. She's never wanted anything from me before tonight. And yet, she's the first woman I've ever considered giving everything to.

"Mmm . . . Hud?" Her sleepy voice soothes my quickly spiraling mind, and I press my lips to the top of her head.

"Sleep, Mads. I've got you."

"Mmm . . ." She rolls over so her face is buried in my chest, and those long lashes kiss her cheeks. She's basically asleep and probably won't remember this in the morning, but I tuck her against me anyway and close my eyes. "I like that."

So do I, Maddie. So do I.

Sunday morning, I wake up to an empty bed and a pit in my stomach.

If she left this house without saying so much as a goodbye, she better get used to my hands on her fucking body because I'm going to spank her ass and then fuck her until she begs me to let her come. Goddammit. The whole *no women leading up to a fight* rule doesn't usually bother me, but this time . . . This time, it's wreaking fucking havoc on my life. A quick look at the clock and I know exactly where my little ball of sunshine is, and ten minutes later, when I find her in front of the television watching the Philly Kings game taking place in London, I smile, knowing I was right.

Her blonde hair is damp and hanging down over a black-and-gold Kings jersey, with *Dixon* stitched in gold across the back and the number 66 beneath it. Judging by the way it swallows her small body, it's obvious she's wearing one of her brother's old jerseys, not something she bought from the store. She's got a needle in her hand but doesn't take her eyes away from the screen until they flash to a commercial.

I'm not sure if I should walk back out and give her space or let her know I'm here, but Maddie takes my choice away when she turns her head to me. "Hey. Sorry. I didn't want to wake you up, but there was no way I was missing this game."

She lifts the jersey and stabs herself with the needle before laying it down on the coffee table, and I have to lean against the couch. "Are you okay? You don't get queasy about needles, do you?"

I groan because yes . . . Yes, I kinda do. "They're not my favorite thing, but I'm fine. I always wondered why you don't have one of those pump things I've seen. Wouldn't that be easier?"

"We tried that a few years ago, but I had a reaction to it, and honestly, I'm so used to this, it doesn't bother me." She picks up a piece of avocado toast. "Want a bite?"

I shake my head.

Maddie shrugs and takes a bite. "How are you feeling? Do you think you'll be okay to go back to training tomorrow?"

"I'll be fine tomorrow. I'm going to make a protein shake. You want one?"

The game comes back on, and she turns back around, effectively ignoring me and letting me know where I rank when her brother is on TV.

And now, I sound like a butt-hurt teenager.

What the fuck?

I need to get back in the gym.

Maddie

Hudson watches most of the game with me, which makes sense. His family owns the team. But I feel like he's watching *me* more than the game, and it's a little unnerving. Especially considering the way last night ended and today started.

It wasn't that I was in his bed.

It wasn't even that I was in his arms, although I would've thought that would be an issue.

Nope.

The issue is that I liked it.

The issue is that I craved it.

Craved him.

The issue at the heart of it all is that last night was the first time I'd fought with anyone in so many years that I couldn't remember the last time I'd done it. The last time I got mad enough to argue. To yell. To take that risk. Because I don't do that. When you're always worried about being shipped off to the next house, you quickly learn to be flexible. To be easygoing and to never argue.

I've had disagreements with Daphne over the years, but we've never actually argued about anything because there was never an issue important enough for me to take that chance. But last night . . . that was important. Because this man is important to me.

And that realization knocks me on my butt, almost as much as the realization that I feel safe with him. That after all these years, I was finally able to let down my carefully constructed walls long enough to let anyone in and fight with them.

No. Not just anyone.

Hudson.

Even when I woke up this morning, it was different. I didn't freak out when I felt his arms around me. I stayed there, soaking it in for a few minutes before I forced myself out of his bed, equal parts shocked and disappointed.

Shocked because I slept through an entire night wrapped in his arms.

Disappointed because it's over.

I'm going home after this game, and we're going back to the way it was before.

It's for the best. Hudson is still Hudson, and I'm still me. We don't work.

But that doesn't make it suck any less.

It might have actually made the whole thing worse. Because I got a tiny little taste of normal. For a few hours, I wasn't broken. But as Brandon's team celebrates their win on the big screen TV, I know my *normal* is ending.

"Guess I'll head home now." I stand, disappointed but determined. "I've already got my bags packed, and you're obviously feeling better." I try to step away, but Hudson gently grabs my wrist. His thumb rests over my wildly beating pulse.

"I am feeling better, Mads. But they still haven't found whoever broke into the gym. Why don't you stay here for another night?" I don't pull away. I don't flinch at his touch, and that, by itself, feels like a win.

His bottomless blue eyes hold me captive, tempting me to agree. But one more night won't change anything. "I've got to get myself ready for the week, Hud. I've got to do laundry and figure out my schedule. And you've got to train. You have a fight in less than a week." With a pit in my stomach, I take a step back.

A blank mask falls over his face as he stands. "Let me get my shoes on, and I'll grab your bags."

"I've got them. They're not heavy." But by the time I get the last word out, Hudson is gone, and I'm left standing there with a sinking feeling.

Maybe I imagined it.

Maybe there wasn't anything between us. Hud's always been a flirt. I guess that's all it was . . . flirting. Because he doesn't do serious. Maybe it's for the best.

CINDER DOESN'T LEAVE my side once she and I walk through the front door of our house. It's like she's out of sorts after only spending a few short days at Hudson's. Like she misses him.

Me too, girl. Me too.

When an incoming FaceTime rings on my MacBook later that night, I'm surprised to see Daphne's face on my screen but more surprised it took her so long to call. "Hey, D. What's up?" She leans forward, and her giant, pregnant boobs almost pop out of her tank top. "Holy heck, Daphne. Put them away before they poke my eyes out."

Max steps up behind his wife and leans over her shoulder. "Blasphemy, Madison. She should never put them away. How's my brother doing?"

Daphne throws her elbow back into Max's side. "Hush, you. Don't go hijacking my conversation."

"Did you really step in between Hudson and another fighter last night, Mads?" Daphne sits back, and Max kneads her shoulders until she moans.

"Oh my God. No moaning, D. Just no," I groan. "And I didn't step in between them so much as I stood in front of Hudson."

"Madison," Max snaps. "Never put yourself between two people who look like they're about to fight. Especially when one of them is Hudson. He can handle himself."

Yeah. I know that now.

I keep that thought to myself, though, and nod my head and watch as Max walks away with Daphne watching his ass the whole time. "Umm . . . D? Do you want to go jump your husband? We can talk later."

She spins around with a sheepish grin on her face. "Nope. I'll do that later. For now, I want to hear about what happened after you left Kingdom last night. Because according to Becket, Hudson looked like he was either going to fuck you or fight you, and you don't look bruised, Mads."

Her entire face lights up, and she shifts on the chair. "Ohh . . . unless your vagina is bruised. Those are the best bruises," she adds wistfully, and I know my face just flushed fifty shades of red.

"No. We didn't . . . It wasn't like that . . . exactly." Oh my God. Why do I get so tongue-tied talking about this?

"Details, please," Daphne insists.

"He was mad at me for getting in the way. Worried I would get hurt. We argued, and it was heated, but Hudson would never lay a hand on me. I don't honestly think the thought would ever even cross his mind." I remember the way his hands held my face, and I swear to God, I can still feel them there.

Daphne giggles. "What is that?" she asks as she points at her screen.

"What?" I ask, growing self-conscious.

"That's the second time your face has gone red in the last two minutes. Spill it, sister."

"Nothing happened, D. But . . ." I run my top teeth over my bottom lip, deciding what I want to tell her. It feels weird, like I'm somehow betraying something precious by talking about last night. "There was something there. Something I'm not ready to talk about yet."

"Okay," she agrees immediately, and I cock my head and stare at her.

"That's it? You're not going to push?"

"When Max and I first got together, you trusted me. You didn't push, and I needed that to figure things out on my own. So, I'm here when you're ready to talk."

"Thanks, D. Talk soon, okay?" She blows me a kiss, and I close my laptop.

I'm done working for the night and have plotted out my schedule for the week.

I've meal-prepped, done my laundry, scheduled a few meetings, and cleaned the house, even though Brandon's cleaning lady will be here Tuesday. Keeping busy was the only thing keeping me close to sane today.

The doorbell rings, and I look at the clock.

Who the heck is here at eight o'clock at night?

After a quick peek through the peephole, I yank the door open. "Hudson? What the heck are you doing here?"

Hud stands on the other side of the door, looking handsome as ever in his black sweats and matching hoodie with a lopsided grin tugging at his lips that vanishes as his eyes sweep over me.

"Mads . . . What are you wearing?" The snow that started falling a few hours ago looks beautiful as it frames him against the light of the house.

I reach forward and grab his arm, pulling him inside and slamming the door shut. "It's freezing outside. Let's keep the cold air out there, okay?" Hud stares at me with wide eyes, and I tilt my head down to confirm I still have my clothes on. "I'm wearing clothes. What are you talking about? You've seen me in less than this when I'm teaching in the gym."

"Tell me you're wearing pants under that," Hudson practically growls his words through clenched teeth.

I lift my oversized Crucible t-shirt to show him the plaid boxers hiding underneath. "I'm wearing shorts, you moron. And my socks go up to my freaking knees. What's the big deal?"

He swallows and looks away before answering, "Not a big deal." Then he walks into my house like he owns the place, looks around for a minute, and stops at the bottom of the steps, where Cinder winds her way through his legs and flicks her tail at him. "Come on."

"Come where?" I'm so confused.

"Lock the door, Madison. Set the alarm, and let's go to bed."

I blink at him a few times, wondering if I hit my head at some point between ending my call with Daphne and answering the door. "You don't live here, Hudson." Despite that, I lock the door and set the alarm, just like he ordered me to, then pad over to him. "Why are you here?"

"I've got to meet Coop for a run before the sun even comes up tomorrow, but I need to know what happens in the next *Harry Potter* movie. I turned it off last night after you fell asleep. So, I figured we could watch it in your room . . . at least until you pass out. Because let's face it, these may be your favorite movies, but they put you to sleep." Hudson says this so matter-of-factly, I stare at him, stunned, for another minute before it dawns on me that I'm relieved he's here.

So instead of overthinking it, I turn off the downstairs light, take the man's hand, and lead him upstairs. When we step into my room, I look at my bed, then back at Hudson, whose huge presence manages to suck all the oxygen from the room. "It's only a queen. Are you even going to fit?"

He kicks off his sneakers and pulls his hoodie over his head. It brings his white undershirt up his chest, and my eyes take the opportunity to soak in those gloriously defined abs before he yanks it back down. "Yup." He moves to the opposite side of my bed and pulls back my comforter. "I'd have figured you for a pink girl, Mads."

My blanket is a pale blue with beautiful golden thread woven through it. I found it at a farmers' market a few years ago and splurged on it immediately. "Well, you'd have figured wrong then, King. I don't like pink." I pick up my phone to plug it into the charger, then look across the bed. "Is your phone charged?"

"Yeah. It's good. I'll just set my alarm. I've gotta get out of here early."

I grab a piece of paper and jot down the alarm code so he can get out in the morning, completely ignoring how strange this is and just going with how happy I am to see him.

Yeah . . . I'm going to have to examine that fact a little harder tomorrow.

For now, I grab the remote and turn off the light as I crawl into bed, not even bothering to act like I'm trying to stay on my side of the bed. I'm proud of myself when I embrace the urge to sit next to him and don't revert to needing space.

Hudson lifts his arm like it's the most natural thing in the world, and I look at him, wondering what it is that makes me trust him not to hurt me. What's different about him from every other man I've ever met in my life?

"You gonna leave me hanging, Mads?" His smile lights up his entire face, and my heart skips a beat.

I slide into him and turn the TV on as I yawn.

Pretty sure I'll never make it to the battle at the end of the movie.

But that's okay. I feel like I might actually be winning my own battle tonight.

HUDSON

I've never been this guy before.
   The one who gets clingy.
Not ever. Not even in high school.

I've never had a girlfriend. Never wanted one. Not that, that's what Maddie is, but it's what she's beginning to feel like. And what shocks the shit out of me at that recognition is that I don't hate that idea. It doesn't scare me. It feels . . . *right*.

I didn't dwell on that realization while I drove over here last night. I just did what I'm good at and followed my gut instinct. It hasn't steered me wrong yet.

She didn't throw me out, like I thought she might.

She didn't give me too hard of a time, like I was sure she would.

She didn't even really hesitate to lay her head against me, which made me feel a little like the grinch whose heart expanded three sizes. It may sound like a ridiculously low bar to set, but for Maddie, I'm willing to take baby steps. Fuck . . . *I* need to take baby steps for myself.

Christ. Cade is gonna kick my ass all over the ring if he finds out I was even thinking this way, with a fight less than a week away. But compared to the other thoughts I was having while Maddie's warm body spent the night wrapped in my arms—with her sweet scent invading my senses and her face tucked against my chest—it was a marathon of self-restraint, having her that close and wanting her that badly but not acting on it.

Not burying myself inside her and showing her how good it'll be between us.

Because what's hitting me like a roundhouse kick is the fact that there will be an *us*.

I have a few more days left of *no women* . . . Pretty sure in some ways, I've already stepped over the line Cade draws in the sand before every fight.

It's never been this hard before now. Before *her*.

When the alarm chimes at five a.m., I reach over, grab my phone from the nightstand, and turn it off, then roll back to my sunshine. She hasn't cracked open an eye, but there's a small smile tugging at her lips. "I've gotta go, sunshine."

"Mmm . . . do you have to?" She nuzzles her face against me.

Okay, now I know she's still asleep.

I lean down and kiss her forehead, like it's the most natural thing in the world, and feel her smile grow instead of her body recoiling. I could get used to this version of Maddie. The affectionate one. The one who doesn't pull back and shy away from me. "I'll see you at the gym tonight."

She hums again, and the sound goes straight to my dick. "Train hard, King." Then with her eyes closed and a beautiful, sleepy look on her face, she pulls the blanket up to her chin, and I force myself to pick up my sweatshirt and sneakers, then head downstairs with a ridiculous smile on my face.

Cinder follows me into the living room and scratches at

the front door before it opens and Brandon Dixon walks into his house.

So much for the good morning.

Dixon is the center for the Philadelphia Kings, and he's one of the best in the league. He's as protective as they come, on and off the field. At an easy six feet, three inches, and probably close to three hundred pounds, he's not a small guy. Not a dumb guy either. Most men would probably find him intimidating.

I'm not most men

I'm also not stupid enough to ignore the fact he just found me coming out of his sister's bedroom.

He drops his duffle bag and closes the door, never taking his eyes off me. "What the fuck are you doing here, Kingston?" After a quick glance at his watch, he groans, "It's five in the fucking morning. Care to explain?"

"Great game yesterday." My smile vanishes, and I cringe.

Bullshitting isn't usually so hard.

He ignores my non-answer and walks into the kitchen without saying a word.

What the hell am I supposed to do? Follow him?

"You want a cup of coffee?" he asks from the other room.

I guess that answers my question.

I step into the kitchen and shove my hands into my pockets, itchy to get the hell out of here. "No thanks, man. I've got to get to training."

"Care to tell me why you're leaving my house at the ass crack of dawn?" He looks around me for something, then adds, "I don't see my sister."

Yeah . . . this looks bad, and I'm not exactly sure how to handle this situation. "She's still sleeping."

"And you were . . . ?" He leaves off the end of the sentence, his question fully implied.

"Listen, I know what this looks like, but—"

Dixon cuts me off, with a hand in the air. "Maddie's a grown woman. I don't need to know what you guys were doing."

Shocked, I can't help myself. "Really?" Seriously, this goes against everything I've ever heard about this guy.

"Do you care about my sister?" He grabs his coffee cup from the machine and downs the piping hot liquid.

"Yeah. I do. But nothing's happening." I leave off the *not yet* because that's between me and her.

"Don't fuck it up."

I'm pretty sure I look at him like he's lost his goddamned mind. "What's the catch? Everyone who knows Maddie knows how protective you are. You find me in your house, and I'm pretty sure it's the first time you've ever found a guy here, and all you're gonna say is *don't fuck it up?*" It doesn't make sense.

"Maddie's not stupid. Hell, she's smarter than me and I'm guessing you too. And she never lets anyone in. If you're in, there's a reason. And if she's going to finally give somebody a chance, at least it's not some weaselly little pencil dick who won't or can't protect her when I'm not around. You can at least keep her safe." Dixon takes a long, slow breath, then grunts. "Looks like you're the lesser of two evils, King." He finishes his coffee, then puts the empty mug in the sink.

"But like I said, don't fuck it up. My sister's been hurt more already than most people will hurt in a lifetime. She deserves better. Question is, are you it?"

I stare at him, wondering where the hell this conversation came from and why Dixon would ever trust me as he leaves me in the kitchen, heading for the stairs. "Lock the door before you leave, Kingston." Then he's gone, and I'm left standing there, trying to figure out what just happened.

My first day back in the gym sucks fucking ass.

Even just a few days off is enough to set you back. It doesn't matter what kind of condition I keep myself in year-round, I still feel the difference. And that's the bitch of choosing this profession. This life. But I've been training for it for years. I'm not about to go soft and hand my title over to Maniac McGuire.

"You've got less than four days to drop fourteen pounds, King. Get in the steam room." Cade turns to Cooper, who's been on my training team for the past two years, "Keep him moving."

Coop just got here a few minutes ago and looks at me like maybe he's rethinking helping today. But he cuts me off before I can say anything. "Shut up and sit in the damn steam room, King."

Once my sauna suit is on with duct tape closing every opening it has, Coop sits across from me, with a pissed-off look on his face.

"Are you constipated or something?" I try to joke, but he just glares.

"You need to focus, King. Are you ready for this fight?"

"A representative from the league stopped by earlier for my drug test. I've gotta drop this weight, but I've had to drop more in less time than this. The Maniac doesn't stand a fucking chance." I fist-bump Coop and get back into position for another round of push-ups, but he doesn't move. Doesn't even say anything. "What else is on your mind, Sinclair?"

"Just keep your head in the game, King."

That pinched fucking look is still on his face. "What are you talking about?"

"Maddie, dickhead. Don't act stupid. I saw you Saturday night. I saw the look on your face. And I'm not talking about the way you were looking at Spider either. You've got a week left. Don't split your focus now." Not many people would have noticed that, but Coop isn't everyone else. He's a former Navy SEAL. This fucker was trained to notice everything.

"What would you have done if somebody said that about Carys?" I lob back at him.

And judging by the way his eye twitches at the mention of his wife, it hit the target. "You can't fucking compare the two," he snaps back at me. "I love my wife. Are you in love with Maddie?"

Well, damn.

That's one way to slam me up against the cage.

Especially since I'm not sure about the answer.

Maddie

"Thanks, D. I'll see you tomorrow at ten to discuss the foundation's push for the food drive and the new year." I end my call with my best friend, with the meeting scheduled for her non-profit's social-media presence and a list of research points I need to dig into later today.

Monday mornings are always housekeeping days for my business, followed by meetings in the afternoon, then a yoga class at Crucible at night. I guess I'm a creature of habit because the routine always calms my restless mind. And I've spent today more on edge than usual.

Last night was so far out of my comfort zone, I should have been crawling out of my skin. I think what's freaking me out the most about it is *I'm not*.

It doesn't even make sense.

But it's occupied all my spare thoughts, so I've been trying to keep myself extra busy today.

It's the only excuse I have for completely zoning out

when my brother apparently came downstairs because when he clears his throat to let me know he's two feet away, I'm pretty sure I jump high enough to hit the ceiling. "What the heck?" I stand and throw my arms around him. "Warn a girl next time. I didn't know you were home."

He holds me tightly to him, and the stress of the morning melts away. "Missed you, Mads."

"I missed you too. But that was an incredible game yesterday. That block you made in the fourth quarter is why you guys won that game. I hope they realize that." Brandon shakes his head at my excitement.

He sits down on the couch and kicks his bare feet up on the ottoman, then smirks. "So . . . I'm gone less than a week, and you're having sleepovers?"

"Excuse me?" I squeak.

Brandon leans forward and waits for me to sit down. But I hold my ground, already uncomfortable with where this conversation is going. "There was a Kingston in my kitchen when I got home this morning. Care to tell me why, *little sister?*"

"I was unaware I needed to clear my friends with you, *big brother*." I plant both hands on my hips and meet his glare, unsure if he's angry or joking.

When his single dimple pops deep in his cheek, I know he's not actually mad.

At least, I think he's not.

"I'm all for you and the girls having sleepovers and pillow fights. All the pillow fights. Maybe add Chloe and Carys's lingerie to the mix too. The more, the merrier. But I wasn't expecting to come home and see one of my team owners strolling out of your bedroom, Madison."

"First, eww. You're disgusting. I've never had a pillow fight in my life"—I grab one of the throw pillows I insisted on after he bought the world's most boring, masculine couch and smack him in the face with it—"until now."

Brandon picks the pillow up and smacks my hip with it. "Damn fucking shame too. You've got some hot friends, and if I block you out of the equation, that's basically most men's fantasies."

"Hey," I bristle, completely unsure of how exactly we got to this point in the conversation. "Are you saying I'm not fantasy material? I mean I might not be a model or anything, but I don't think I'm hard on the eyes either, you jerk."

He yanks me down by the arm until I'm sitting next to him on the couch. "I'm not a Lannister, Mads. Incest doesn't do it for me. And if some guy said he was saving you for spank-bank material, I'd have to kill him."

"Wait . . . *spank bank?*" I scrunch up my face, utterly grossed out. "Please freaking stop. I'm begging you. I can handle you talking about fantasies—to an extent. I don't want to know my friends are in your *spank bank*."

But when he laughs at me, I remember how the conversation started. "Stop distracting me, Brandon. I'm a grown woman. I run a successful business, and I've managed to navigate life just fine, thank you very much. I don't need your permission to spend time with whomever I want. Man or woman." That might have been more convincing if I didn't have to remind him I'm a grown woman.

"I wasn't saying you needed to ask for permission. I was saying I was surprised to see Hudson Kingston this morning. That's all. I'm not used to guys sleeping here." He throws his arm across the back of the couch and tugs on my hair.

"Watty crashes here all the time," I pout.

"Watty's crashing on the couch after too many beers. He's not telling me he left my baby sister sleeping in her room. Just promise me you're being safe."

"Oh. My. God." I hide my face in my hands, remembering ten years ago when he asked me that the first time. "Are you really giving me the birds and the bees talk . . . *again?*"

"Maddie . . ." He waits for me to look at him.

"Not that you deserve to hear this, but we just slept. We turned on a movie and fell asleep, fully freaking clothed, Brandon."

"That doesn't sound like you."

My eyes go huge and bug the heck out of my head. "What?"

My brother practically stumbles over himself to fix his words. "I mean, you let him get that close? Close enough to fall asleep in your room? That doesn't sound like something you'd usually do."

"It doesn't, does it?" And with a deep breath, I fill him in on everything that's happened since last Thursday night.

The break-in.

Hudson's knee.

The crazy confrontation at Kingdom.

All of it.

When I'm finished spinning the crazy week, Brandon sits back on the couch and just stares at me until I finally break under his intense scrutiny. "I knew you'd be mad I didn't tell you right away, but I wanted you focused on your game, not me. I was fine."

And then he breaks, jumping to his feet, enraged. "You're not going to Crucible. You don't need that fucking job, and Cade St. James obviously can't keep you safe."

Slowly, I stand and take his hand in mine. "It was a break-in, Brandon. It could have happened anywhere."

"Fine. Then I'm taking you to your class tonight, and I'm staying until you're done. I don't want you there alone. Get your stuff." Brandon's dark eyes harden.

"Aren't you overreacting a bit here?"

"Chop, chop, Mads. We're leaving in ten minutes." He starts to walk away, and I want to scream.

"Brandon," I call after him. "Don't you have to go to the stadium today?"

He doesn't even turn around. "Nope. Bye week. We've got the day off. Lucky you."

Yeah . . . lucky me.

MADDIE

I agreed to let Brandon drive me to Crucible, fully aware and yet still aggravated by the fact there was no way I was going to win that argument. I'm not a pushover, but I learned early on to pick my battles. And judging by the fact he hasn't said two words since I got into the car, this wasn't a battle worth fighting. I'm saving my energy for when we get to the gym. If I can't get him to go home at that point, then I'll go to war. Until then, I pull my phone from my bag and open the group chat with the girls.

MADDIE

Brandon's home, and he's lost his freaking mind. Are any of you coming to class tonight? I might need backup.

DAPHNE

Why? So I can look like a beached whale next to all of you? Ummm . . . nope.

CARYS

You're pregnant. You'd look beautiful.

CHLOE

Kiss ass!

CARYS

Pucker up, baby.

DAPHNE

One of these days, you're going to say fucking instead of freaking, and we're all going to know you mean business, Mads.

MADDIE

La la la . . . I'm ignoring you, D.

DAPHNE

Very mature, Mads.

CHLOE

Why'd the big guy lose his mind? Wait . . . Oh shit. Did Hudson finally pop your cherry? Did Dixon walk in? I mean, girl, the way Hudson was looking at you Saturday night was hot enough to burn Kingdom to the ground.

MADDIE

Nope. My cherry is still firmly in place. He's pissed because I just told him about the break-in, and now he wants to play bodyguard or something.

DAPHNE

Oh damn.

CHLOE

Ohhh . . . I'm coming to class. I want to see this.

CARYS

Me too.

DAPHNE

Someone FaceTime me so I can see too.

CAGED

MADDIE

> You guys are no help.

When we park in front of Crucible, after the longest seven-minute drive of my life, I get out of the car and successfully fight the overwhelming urge to slam the door behind me like a brat. But wow, that urge was strong.

"Madison." But Brandon *does* slam his door, and I whirl around, ready to scream.

I make sure to check myself and keep my voice calm. *Go me.* "What, Brandon? I let you drive me here. I don't have to be happy about it. This is my job."

"You don't even need this job. You could quit tomorrow, and you'd be fine." Brandon's glare grows. "I'm not going to apologize for being worried about you. I want to know what's going on, and I want to talk to Cade." He takes a step before I move between him and the front door.

"Could you please trust me . . . just this one time, trust me to take care of myself?" I lift my chin, in an attempt to be stubborn, but I'm not sure whether I'm getting anywhere or failing miserably.

Pretty sure I'm failing.

With a shake of his head, he moves around me and storms through the front door, more like a father than a big brother, and I'm left standing outside with my blood boiling.

This is what I get for humoring his constant need to be overprotective.

I tilt my head up to the darkening sky and take a deep breath, then blow it out and watch it dance through the ice-cold air, already so over this night. When I finally push through the front doors into the busy gym, the soundtrack of metal weights clanging against the mats, Avenged Sevenfold thrumming through the speakers, and Hudson's team yelling instructions at him while he spars in the cage, is like music to my ears.

I missed this.

I love my social-media business. I love my clients and the flexibility of the work. But there's something about being in this gym . . . My muscles loosen, my mind clears, and I'm centered in a way that comes naturally here.

Awareness prickles my skin, and like a magnetic force is pulling me toward him, I turn to the cage and find Hudson staring my way, right before his sparring partner, Jax, knocks him down. "Pay attention, asshole," is shouted in the cage, and Hudson hops right back up and shakes it off.

Oops. With a shake of my head, I turn around and decide to ignore my brother—who's already deep in conversation with Cade next to the cage—bypassing everyone on my way to the locker room. It only takes a minute to pull off the sweats and hoodie I've layered over my yoga gear and tuck them away in my locker. With a chill still running over my skin, I leave my tank top on over my sports bra and adjust my boobs.

I stand there for a minute, looking at myself in the mirror and fortifying my walls so when I walk back out there, I've got the strength to tell Brandon to go home and let me work.

I know he's going to fight me.

But I *think* I'm ready to deal with it.

Only when I step back into the front of the gym, he's not there. I cross the room and pull myself up to sit on the counter behind Imogen. "Do I even want to know where my brother went?"

She looks up from the desk and swivels in her chair with an evil grin on her face, then pulls the pen out of the messy bun on top of her head and points it toward the cage.

I follow her direction, but Brandon isn't there. And

neither is Hudson. "English, Gen. I have no idea what you're trying to tell me."

"Hudson came over to talk to Cade and Dixon a few minutes ago. Hud told your brother he'd stick around for your class and drive you home. Then Dixon agreed and left." She snaps her gum, then blows a giant pink bubble in my face.

A finger reaches over my shoulder, popping it. "Don't you have work to do?" Cade asks his sister.

She stands from her chair and smacks a notebook against his chest. "Nope. I'm done for the day. See ya tomorrow." She wiggles her fingers at me and disappears into the back of the gym.

"Maddie," Cade starts, but I stop him.

"Listen, Cade, I'm sorry about my brother. I just filled him in on what happened, and I guess he felt a certain way about it." What the heck? I don't even know if that made sense.

"Stop, Mads. It's fine. Until we know exactly what's going on, no one is going to be alone in this gym. That's the new rule. Safety in numbers." He puts the notepad down on the desk and picks up a business card. "The detective from last week stopped by today. They don't have any new information on the break-in, but they do have extra patrol cars driving by."

"Okay. But really, I'm not scared to be here alone, Cade." I hate the idea that someone else will have to take time away from their lives and their families three nights a week to babysit me.

Cade chuckles. "Yeah. Pretty sure that won't be an issue." He looks over my head, and from the way my skin warms, I know exactly who's just walked back into the room. "The fight's in five days, Maddie. Just do me a favor and make sure he stays focused until then. After that, he's all yours."

My eyes snap so far open I think they might be detaching

from their sockets. "What?" I look over my shoulder and watch Hud climb back into the black metal cage. "We're just friends."

"Five days, Madison." Cade's voice is firm as he walks away, and I burn with a daunting mix of humiliation and something else.

Something stronger.

Something I can't put my finger on, but it's right there, hiding under the surface.

And it's scarier than any break-in could ever be.

Hudson

I don't mind the sauna most days. It serves a purpose, like everything else. Some guys love it, and some guys hate it. To me, it's a tool. Weigh-ins are Friday. So for now, it's a necessary evil I'll be using a few times a day, all fucking week. But I'm fucking tired at this point in the day. I've just closed my eyes for a minute, lying back on the bench, when the door slams open and Cade walks in.

"Keep your head in the fucking game, King." His frustrated tone is like sandpaper rubbing my skin raw.

I slowly sit up and wipe the sweat from my face with my towel, then toss it to the bench. "It's in the game, Saint," I growl back, tired of everyone telling me the same fucking thing today.

"You're not fucking focused, and that's never an option. Especially not now. You get distracted—you'll get hurt. And my wife won't just kill you, she'll kill *me* too. You should be going home, icing your body, and going to bed. Not staying here to play bodyguard to Madison Dixon."

I stand from the bench and step up to Cade. "Watch it,

Saint. I love you like a brother, but you're walking a fine line."

"That's what I thought," he grinds through gritted teeth. "Days, man. You've got days left. Don't lose now because you're splitting focus. The rules are there for a reason. And one more week isn't making a difference after three goddamn years."

This man has been my coach, my friend . . . damn, he's my brother-in-law, and I respect the hell out of him. I have for a decade. But he's not making sense. "I don't even know what you're trying to get at."

"Did you know your sister and I used to wonder what the hell was going on with you and Imogen? We took bets on whether you guys were a thing and were just keeping it to yourselves, or if you really were just friends. Wanna know when we stopped?"

What the hell? "When you pulled your heads out of your asses and figured out that we're friends? That I love Imogen like I love my sisters." Swear to God, I look at Cade like he's losing his mind. "Which one of us has spent too much time sweating it out today, Saint? You're not making sense."

"It was when Madison Dixon walked through the front door of Crucible. We've all seen it for years. You two are the ones who haven't." His eyes narrow on me. "We both know she's got some issues to work through. And seriously, man . . . I don't want you to miss what's right in front of your face. But I swear to God . . . One fucking week. Defend your title. Win the fucking fight. Then go get your girl."

He stands there for another minute. I don't know if he's waiting for an answer or expecting a fight, but when he doesn't get either, his stance eases, and he grabs the door. "Jax is gonna close the gym up tonight, so once her class is done, I want you to take her home and then ice. Got it?" He takes a step back, his hand still on the open door. "I'm outta here for the night. See you tomorrow."

I catch a glimpse of pretty blonde hair as the door swings closed behind Cade and push it back open. *Motherfucker.* Maddie is standing in the locker room on the other side of the sauna door, and judging by the confused look on her face, she just got an earful. "Mads . . ." I take a step toward her, but she backs up.

"Sorry." She stumbles backward. "I was just . . ." Maddie looks around and takes another step until she's backed against one of the lockers. "My class is about to start, and I wanted to thank you for offering to take me home. But Chloe's here, so I'm going to catch a ride with her."

I move in front of her and cup her beautiful face in both my hands.

Her eyes dart to my mouth and then up to my eyes, but she doesn't pull away, even if she's thinking about it.

"Let me take you home, sunshine." My muscles tense as she licks her lips.

"Hudson . . ."

I slide my fingers into her hair. "Madison." She nuzzles into my hand, and I feel like I just won the greatest title fight ever with that simple move.

I move slowly enough for her to stop me if she wants, then press my lips to the top of her head. "I'm going to run on the treadmill. Go teach your class. I'll meet you when it's over."

When her dazed sapphire eyes lift to meet mine, there's no mistaking the want that's replaced the indecision I've come to expect. "You better get out there, sunshine."

A pretty flush crawls up her skin, and a small, timid smile graces her full lips before she walks away, leaving me to watch her go.

I stand there for a minute, thinking about what Cade said

about the way things changed when Maddie came to work at Crucible. I noticed her back then, but it was different. She's gorgeous, and so sweet. And that smile of hers is always welcoming everyone in, but only so far. And I'm not sure when it happened, but I want more.

I want more of the Maddie she doesn't show everyone else. The one she's started to give me, piece by piece. I want to know why she hides it. Why she doesn't want to be touched. Why she runs.

I want the real Maddie.

The one no one else knows.

I want her to let me in.

WHEN I HEARD Cade and Dixon discussing the break-in earlier, I knew Maddie's brother was pissed.

Of course he'd be.

I'm not sure if he was mad because no one had told him, but he was definitely furious that it happened in the first place.

Join the club.

His plan was to wait for her tonight, and for her to cancel her other two classes this week until the cops found the guy.

Yeah, Maddie's gonna be pissed when she hears that.

But he backed off when I told him I'd stay and keep an eye on everything, then drive her home. I think that's what set Cade off. What the hell am I talking about? He's always edgy around a fight. I think it drives him nuts that I'm not. I don't let it stress me out. This is my norm. I work for it all year, not just eight weeks beforehand. I guess you could call it my zen.

This thing with Maddie . . . This is the first time in all my years of fighting for Crucible that a woman's ever been in my life before a fight. And I get that's freaking him the fuck out, but he's out of his mind if he thinks I'm backing off now.

Not when I'm finally interested in seeing where this thing between us could go.

By the time Maddie's class is wrapping up, I've already got my stuff together and am sitting on the front desk, waiting for her. Her girls close ranks around her as the rest of the class spills out into the parking lot. Carys and Chloe block my view of the tiny blonde whose got the power to destroy me in ways no opponent ever has.

I learned something new tonight. There's a certain treadmill that gives me the perfect view of the yoga class. That also meant Maddie could see me watching her if she turned around. I know she felt it because more than once, she'd look back over her shoulder and smile. And damn, that smile did things to me.

She makes me feel like a fucking teenager, nervous to ask the pretty girl out.

And I wasn't even nervous when I was a teenager. What the fuck?

She finally pulls away from her friends and walks by me into the locker room without glancing my way. I hop off the desk and catch up to Carys and Chloe as they roll up their mats. "How are we doing, ladies?"

Chloe crosses her arms in front of herself and eyes me up and down. "What are your intentions toward our friend, Kingston?"

It takes every ounce of strength in me not to laugh. "Dude. Even Dixon didn't ask me that this morning."

Carys mirrors Chloe's stance. "Well, we're not Dix. And we want an answer. You two have been spending an awful lot of time together."

I smile at these women, secretly in awe of them protecting their friend. "My intentions are between Maddie and me, ladies." My smile stretches across my face when they both roll their eyes. "Sorry."

Carys grabs Chloe's mat from her and walks away, leaving Chloe, who's giving me a hard stare. "Are you gonna hurt her, King?" She cocks a perfectly sculpted eyebrow, like I should be scared of her. This tiny woman has bigger balls than most men I know.

"What do you think?"

She doesn't look impressed. "I think you're a manwhore, and our friend *isn't*."

"I'm not really into men, so that's a good thing," I try to joke. But she doesn't look impressed. "Listen, because I'm only going to say this once. Don't believe everything you read in the papers. I've known you since you were a twelve-year-old kid, taking your first judo lesson. Do you really think I'd hurt her?"

She thinks about it for a second before letting out a quiet huff. "Fine. But I'm watching you."

"Good." I grab her shoulders and guide her to the door. "Now get out of here, so I can drive a pretty girl home. Okay?"

"Smooth, King. Real smooth." She points two fingers at her eyes, then at me. "Best behavior, King."

I nod in agreement as Carys and she leave the gym, then turn to find Maddie walking my way.

"Where are the girls?" she asks as she shoulders her gym bag.

I reach out and take it from her, then open the front door. "Looks like I'm driving you home after all, sunshine."

She gets into the passenger side of my SUV and reaches over to unlock my door. "Do you ever get told no?"

My arm brushes against hers as I slide behind the wheel, and a frisson of electricity courses down my spine. "Only by you, Mads."

HUDSON

With just a few days left before the fight, training starts earlier and lasts longer. But that doesn't mean it's all day. So, with my first break between sessions, I grab my phone to get out of the gym and away from everyone for a couple of hours.

I haven't seen my sister Lenny in a few days. My siblings and I try to do some form of family dinner once a week, if we can. Whether that's a Sunday night at the Kings games or all of us picking a night to watch the Revolution play during the season, we still try. Occasionally, we actually manage to get together at Dad's old house, where his final wife, Ashlyn, and our youngest sister, Madeline, still live. But we skipped family dinner altogether last week, since so many of us spent the weekend in London watching the Kings game. I wasn't disappointed about missing that trip.

After I make a pit stop at Amelia's bakery to grab something for Len, I head to her house. When I walk through her front door, I notice Lenny's gray eyes look like she's gone a few rounds in the ring with one of my opponents and lost.

Of course, that's not what it is because long before I'd

ever get the opportunity to destroy anyone who hurt my sister, Len's husband, Sebastian, would have killed any man who even considered laying a hand on her.

According to the family group text, my nine-month-old nephew, Maverick, has another ear infection and has gone on a sleep strike. Which means his momma isn't getting any sleep either.

I hold up the cup carrier I'm hiding behind my back and smile, knowing the large coffee and bag of muffins should at least help a little. "I come bearing caffeine and muffins from Sweet Temptations." And maybe an ulterior motive, but she doesn't need to know that.

"Shh . . . Maverick's sleeping in the swing. If you wake him up, I swear to God, you're taking him home with you, Hudson." Scolding complete, she lifts up on her toes and kisses my cheek. "But seriously, you know you're my favorite brother."

I hand Lenny the coffee. "Sure I am."

Don't get me wrong. I love being Len's favorite brother. Considering there's five of us, that title is hard-won. We've always been close, and it's a title I cherish. But right now, she'd say that to anyone who walked through the door with coffee.

Lenny grabs the bag of muffins from the counter, then sits down on a kitchen chair and kicks up her legs to rest on the one across from her before she sniffs the bag. "Our sister is a goddess."

"Hey." I pull out the chair next to her and sit. "Amelia's great and all, but I'm the one who brought you sustenance. She only made it."

Her tired eyes roll before she picks her muffin and throws the bag at my head. "I said you were my favorite. What more do you want from me?"

I catch the bag, stick my nose in it, and inhale deeply.

Then I push it aside.

"Just eat one, Hud. You know you want to."

"Training camp, remember? I've got a fight in four days." I pat my abs and ignore the growl coming from her. "No sugar. You know the rules."

"Why are you here and not at the gym then?" She rips off a chunk of the cinnamon swirl goodness and pops it into her mouth, then moans.

"Save it for Bash, Len. I don't need to know what that sounds like." I lean out of the way when she tries to smack me. "I was already there this morning, and I've got to be back later today."

Maverick picks that moment to let us know he's awake with a pathetic whimper, and one look at Len tells me she's about to burst into tears right behind him. I push her coffee closer to her and stand. "You stay here. I've got him."

An exhausted smile pulls at her lips as she whispers—"Definitely my favorite brother"—while I walk out of the room.

When I stop in front of the swing, Len's lazy bulldog is laying at the foot of the baby swing, snoring. He's completely ignoring my chunky little nephew, who stops mid-scream and stares at me. Tear-soaked dark-brown eyes blink before I unbuckle him from the seat and scoop him up. "Mav, my main man. Where's your binky, dude?" I search the cushioned seat for the green pacifier, then stuff my finger in the hollow end, and plunk it back into his mouth, making sure to rub his gums the way Bash showed me. "Come on, dude. Your momma is going on strike if you don't let her sleep soon." He curls into my chest and closes his eyes, revealing the fat, wet teardrops sticking to his long lashes.

"You're so good with him, Hud."

I turn to find my sister watching me. "Yeah well, I get to

give him back at night, Len. It's way easier to be the cool uncle than the tired parent."

She takes a step toward me, then runs her hand over Mav's back. "At some point, you're going to love someone so much, you'll refuse to let go."

"It's not like I don't want that. I just haven't found it yet, Len." My confession is quiet, so I don't upset the ticking time bomb in my arms, but it's true, nonetheless. No one has ever held my interest for more than a night or two.

But even as I think that, I know it's a lie.

I'd love to have what some of my siblings have found. But I honestly didn't know if it was in the cards for me. Not until now. I'm pretty sure my chance has been right in front of my face, and I just needed to open my damn eyes.

Maverick's breathing evens out, but I don't put him down. Not yet. I want to make sure Len gets a few minutes to rest. "Is Bash at the stadium?"

Her husband is a monster on our football team.

"Yeah. They got back from London really early yesterday, so we took the day off together. But we ended up at the pediatrician's office in the afternoon." I follow her back into the kitchen and watch her inhale her coffee. "Did you really just stop by to check on me and bring me coffee?"

Did I?

I stand there with my hand spread wide over Mav's back, debating how I want to answer her question. But I don't have to debate for long.

"Are you going to tell me what's going on with you and Maddie Dixon?" Lenny picks up her muffin and tears another piece off. When I don't answer her right away, she tosses the piece at my head. "Word travels fast, Hudson. Especially when your coach is married to our sister." She tsks at me a few times, with a cocky expression. "He's not happy with you. Says you picked a shit week to decide you're ready to claim your girl."

When my mouth drops open, Lenny smiles. "His words. Not mine. So, tell me again, Hud. Why are you here?"

"Don't ever let anyone tell you you're not the smartest sibling, Len." I sit back down and press a kiss to Mav's big old head. "How did you know Bash was worth the fight?" I ask, then shake my head. "That's not what I meant..."

"Stop. I know what you mean, and I was there. I know I had to fight for my husband. But he was worth it. It was like it was something I knew deep down. There wasn't any one thing. It was everything." Her tired eyes rest on my sleeping nephew, and her whole body relaxes. "As soon as I realized that, I knew I was ready to dig my heels in and refuse to let go."

She crosses the room and refills her coffee cup from the pot brewing on her counter. "Listen to me, big brother. Dad did a number on all of us, in one way or another. But just because he couldn't keep it in his pants, and fell in and out of love more often than most people change their underwear, doesn't mean any of us have to be that way. I honestly think because of that, none of us will be like him. Bash is it for me. He's the love of my life. I don't know what I'd do without him."

"How long did it take you to figure that out?"

"A week. Maybe less. But there's no rule book here, Hud. Bash had his own issues to deal with, and from what I've heard, so does Maddie." She sips her coffee and hums happily to herself. "If you're looking for a rule book to follow, you're going to be disappointed. It looks different for everyone. But seriously, if you're here asking these questions, I think you already know your answer."

Maverick buries his face against my neck and whimpers, so Lenny takes him from me and pats his bottom.

"Somebody needs a diaper change. Wanna help, Uncle Hud?"

"That's all you, Len. I've got to get back to the gym." I stand from the chair and drop a kiss on her head. "Any chance we can keep this talk between us?"

The little brat laughs. "Not a chance. We were all taking bets on who you'd go to. Honestly, I thought it would be Max."

"You coming to the fight Saturday night?" I ask as she follows me to the door.

"Wouldn't miss it, big brother. Love you."

A sound comes out of Maverick, followed by a smell I wouldn't have expected from a baby. "Yeah . . . I'm out. See ya, Len."

"Coward," she calls back.

Ha. That'll be the day.

Maddie

Tuesday afternoon, I finish up my meetings a little late and rush into the house to change for the gym. In hindsight, I really should have been paying closer attention. A scream is ripped from me as a man pops out in front of me. Instinct kicks in, and I smack him with my computer.

I guess I should have waited a minute before I did that because Brandon's best friend and Kings teammate, Watkins, is now curled in a ball on the floor, cupping his hand between his legs and groaning.

"Shoot." I squat down next to Watty. "Did I knee you in the nuts too?"

He shakes his head in response and rolls away from me when I lay my hand on his back. "I'm so sorry. But what the heck were you doing scaring me like that?"

"What the hell?" Brandon stops at the bottom of the stairs and looks between Watty and me, then doubles over laughing. "Don't break him, Mads. We need him on Sunday."

I flip him the bird and offer Watkins my hand while he fights his way back onto his feet, eyeing me like I'm going to attack again. "*Shoot*, Mads?" His voice is hoarse and clipped. "Seriously? *Shoot*? You kicked me in the junk, and *shoot* is the best you got?"

He walks gingerly into the kitchen and helps himself to the trusty bag of peas in the freezer, then joins Brandon on the couch and shoves the peas down the front of his gym pants.

My brother hands him the Xbox remote with a scowl. "Throw them out when you're done, asshole. I don't want to ice up later with produce that's touched your balls."

I drown the two of them out and slip my heels off, moaning, now that I can finally feel my toes again. Why do cute shoes always cause so much pain?

"Mads," Brandon looks away from the game they've queued up on the flat screen and waits until I stop walking. "I'm dropping you off at Crucible tonight, and Hudson's bringing you home."

Maybe it's because I'd already kneed Watkins tonight, but I'm feeling a little extra ragey. Or maybe it's just that the last of my carefully held patience has finally snapped. Either way, the result is the same.

I snap.

Well, actually . . . I throw.

A shoe.

Oh my God.

I just threw a shoe.

At my brother's head.

And it bounces off him. Well, off his forehead, to be exact. Oh, thank goodness the heel didn't get him. I stand perfectly still—in complete shock that I just did that—until he stands up, yelling. That's when my anger comes back in full force.

"What the hell, Maddie? You hit me with your fucking shoe." He waves the black patent-leather heel around in the air as a lump quickly forms on the front of his head.

"I'm done, Brandon. I'm done. I'm not a child, and I'm tired of you treating me like one. And you know what? It's my own fault for letting you think you've had the final say in my life for so long. Because guess what?" My entire body shakes, I'm so mad right now.

Mad at him.

Mad at me.

Mad at Watty for being here to witness my meltdown.

"Maddie . . ." Brandon starts, fury lacing his tone, but my phone chimes, cutting him off.

I yank it out of my bag and stare at the text on the screen for a second before walking over to Brandon and grabbing my heel out of his hand. I slip both torture devices back on my feet and grab my bag.

"What are you doing?" He eyes me, confused while Watty looks between us like he's watching a real-life soap opera.

"Daphne just went into labor. I'm meeting her at the hospital." Brandon stands, like he's going to come with me, but I stop him. "I'll call you when the baby's here. Don't come now."

A wave of pain washes over his face. Daphne is his friend too, but she's not going to want to see him now. And I certainly don't want to be around him tonight. "Be safe," he tells me as I pull open the door. I don't bother to answer as I slam it shut behind me.

BELLA MATTHEWS

I CALLED Cade on my way to the hospital and canceled my class for the night. He'd already heard the news from Scarlet and told me not to worry about it. It's hard to believe this is my second time here in less than a week. But tonight is for a much happier reason.

When I walk into the fancy waiting room in the labor and delivery wing of Kroydon Hills Hospital, Scarlet, and Becket are already here, but they're the only Kingstons present.

That won't last long.

Within an hour, they're all here. Everyone but Cade and Hudson. Even Amelia's husband, who isn't exactly big on public gatherings, sits next to his wife, who was just here giving birth to their daughter a few months ago.

Once Max frantically pushes through the doors—his blond hair pushed away from his face, looking crazy, and his white dress shirt, which had been perfectly pressed when I saw him earlier but now a wrinkled mess—I know Daphne is ready. When he calls my name, I'm more than a little relieved to be getting out of the fishbowl of Kingstons I'm currently in.

I know Daphne wants me with her for her labor. It's part of her birth plan. She doesn't have any real family of her own, but Carys, Chloe, and I are all she needs, especially considering she has enough in-laws to fill their own football stadium.

I still can't believe that I get to be here for this with my best friend as we walk along the hospital corridor. "Are you hanging in there, Max?"

This normally unshakable man looks completely undone under the humming fluorescent lights. "You get nine months to get ready for this. You read all the books you can get your hands on. You talk to your sisters and your friends who've all had kids. You hear all the stories, and you think you're ready. They all say that once the baby is born, it's like walking around with your heart outside your body."

We turn a corner toward the hall full of delivery rooms, and he points at one a few feet away. "But nobody tells you what it's like to know your wife is in pain and there's nothing you can do about it."

We stop outside Daphne's room, and Max's dark eyes boring into me remind me so much of his brother's that they seem to soothe my nerves. "I need her to be okay, Maddie." He wraps an arm around my shoulder, and I force myself not to pull away.

"She will be, Max. She's the strongest person I know."

He must like that because a shaky smile pulls at his lips right before we walk into D's room. I was expecting her to be a mess, but that's never been Daphne's way. With tears filling her eyes, she reaches out her hand, and I take it. "Sorry for making you wait." She laughs and gestures around her. "They had to hook me up to all of this."

"You doing okay, D?" I gently brush her hair out of her face. "Need anything?"

"I'm okay for now." She looks me over, then shrugs. "They said it could be a while. I should have told you, you had time to change."

I kick my heels off and set them against the wall, then bite my lip and hold back a silent laugh when I think about hitting Brandon with one of them earlier.

"Spill it, sister. What's that smile about?"

A little embarrassed, I manage to tell D what happened with my brother earlier without sounding too much like a complete psychopath. At least I do, in my opinion. I'm not quite sure what Max thinks because the smart man keeps it to himself. And when a contraction has Daphne gripping both our hands tight a few minutes later, my confession is long forgotten.

Eventually a nurse comes in with a pair of dark-blue hospital socks with little grippers on the bottom to slip on over my pantyhose.

"Damn girl, you look hot," Daphne snickers, looking me over.

"Yeah, yeah, yeah." I mean, my black stockings with the seam up the back of my legs seemed like a good idea when I was getting dressed earlier today. Now, not so much. But how was I to know that I'd be in labor with my best friend?

Seven hours and thirty-five minutes later, to be exact, Serena Kingston is born, screaming her way into the world. She's a tiny, little thing, with an adorable button nose, a strong set of lungs, and a purplish shade of red covering her small body.

And this little girl is the most perfect thing I've ever seen.

As the nurse brings Serena to Daphne's chest, Max leans his head against hers, and they share quiet words meant to only be heard by their new family.

Without another thought, I snag my heels and walk over to the door to quietly duck out, but Daphne catches me before I make my escape. "Love you, Mads. Thank you for being here."

I hold tight to the emotion clogging in my throat. "There's no place I'd rather be."

Daphne swallows. "Will you share the news with anyone who might still be waiting out there?"

"Tell them to come back tomorrow." Max looks at his wife with so much adoration in his eyes, tears burn the back of my lids. "Tonight's just for us."

I grab my bag from the chair, slip my shoes inside and smile. "Love you guys. I'll be back in the morning."

The crowd in the waiting room has dwindled down to just the Kingston siblings. The spouses are gone, probably to take care of their own kids. But these brothers and sisters aren't leaving until they know what's happening with their brother's family.

I ignore most of them and find Hudson, who stands from his chair as soon as he sees me.

The overwhelming emotions of the day pull me under, and I walk right into his open arms, close my eyes, and take a deep breath. I soak in his strength, stealing some for myself before I look up at everyone, suddenly aware of what I just did. I try to pull back, but Hudson wraps his arms around me and gently squeezes.

"It's a girl," I announce to the room. "Serena Kingston. Six pounds, four ounces. She's got a full head of blonde hair and a great set of lungs. Max asked me to let you all know that Daphne and Serena are perfect, but they're exhausted and want everyone to come back tomorrow."

The room is filled with voices and commotion as everyone celebrates the good news.

But Hudson never looks away from me. "Are you okay?"

I manage to answer through a yawn. "I'm good. Just tired."

"Can I drive you home?" Hud tucks a lock of my no doubt messy hair behind my ear, and those cobalt blue eyes seem to stare into my soul.

It's my undoing. It's . . . it's too much and not at all enough.

"Any chance I could crash at your place tonight? I got into a stupid fight with my brother earlier. I'm exhausted, and I—"

"I've got you, sunshine. Leave your car here, and we'll get it in the morning." He takes my hand in his, and I don't pull it away. And somewhere deep in the recesses of my brain, I realize I don't want to.

My eyes stay glued to where his fingers are laced with mine while he says goodnight to the horde of Kingstons still dominating the room.

It's not until we get into his SUV that he looks over at me with a funny expression on his face. "Madison."

I lift my head at his use of my full name.

"Why aren't you wearing any shoes?"

Once I start laughing, it feels like I can't stop—like a damn broke at some point, and the water has been trickling through all day, wearing away at the once small hole. But I can't plug it back up anymore. It's too overwhelming, and my emotions and control are flowing through with no chance of stopping them now. Tears leak from my eyes, and my side hurts by the time my laughter dies down.

Then I look at Hudson.

Really look at him.

No man should look this good this late in the day.

Like a Greek god with sexy scruff dusting his chiseled jaw. His blond hair is messy and falling into his eyes, looking like it's been tugged on for hours. And for just one moment, I imagine what that would feel like.

If I was the one tugging on his hair.

What would that stubble feel like against my skin.

My neck.

My thighs.

"Take me home, King."

HUDSON

"*Take me home, King.*" Those words send a jolt through my body and straight to my dick, whether she meant them *that* way or not.

Maddie crosses her smooth stocking-covered legs and leans her head back against the seat, then pulls her phone from her bag to show me a picture Daphne just sent of my newest niece. She's beautiful. Almost as beautiful as the woman sitting next to me.

"Wanna tell me what happened between you and Dixon?" She doesn't answer. Just shakes her head no.

Okay then.

"Did you get to train tonight, or did you skip it and come right to the hospital?" *Really?* She's going to make small talk?

I'll humor her for now. "I finished the session. We go light tomorrow, then I cut any remaining weight on Thursday. Weigh-ins happen Friday afternoon."

"Are you ready?" Her look of concern catches me off guard.

"Yeah, sunshine. I'm good. Just a few more pounds to cut,

and everything's done." I train hard all year long, so these weeks are only a little longer than normal for me.

Her stare is almost unnerving as we turn on to the back roads of Kroydon Hills. "Hud . . . how did you get into MMA? I mean, you're a Kingston. How in the world did you end up fighting in a cage for a living?"

And there it is.

There's my *in*.

The *in* I've been waiting for. "I'll make you a deal. A question for a question."

"What?" The word is clipped as she shuts down, but I refuse to let that happen.

"For every question you ask, I get to ask you one too." This might be my first real chance to force my way past some of her walls. "I won't push. If you don't want to answer, you don't have to."

She plays with the hem of her dark gray dress before agreeing. "Fine," she huffs. "But I'm not answering any questions until we're in your house. I don't want to feel like I'm trapped in this car."

"No problem. What's your first question?" I volley back to her.

I quickly look her way and see a frustrated expression tightening her face. "I already asked it. How did you end up being a professional MMA fighter? Why that instead of the family business?"

"Short answer first . . . I hated school," I tell her honestly.

"What?" she asks.

"I hated school. It was never easy for me, and I was never as good as Sawyer or Lenny. My parents didn't figure out I was dyslexic until I was in sixth grade, and by then, I'm pretty sure they thought it was ADD. Instead of medicating me, Lenny's mom signed me up for karate. She thought it might help me focus."

"Why Lenny's mom?"

"Once my mom divorced Dad, she checked out. She collected her check every month from different European countries. Sawyer and I barely ever saw her while we were growing up. Len and Jace's mom was way more of a mother to us than ours ever was." My mom was wife number two of four. Dad didn't even marry Amelia's mom.

"Okay, so twelve-year-old Hudson starts karate, then what?" She smiles at me while we're stopped at a red light. Damn, that smile. Her dimples sit deep in her cheeks, and my chest expands. Men have died protecting less than what she's giving me right now.

Because this . . . this is the real Maddie.

"Basically, I loved it. I begged Kristen—that's Lenny and Jace's mom—I begged her to let me take judo, too, because the owner's son was teaching it, and he seemed larger than life. And if you ever tell Cade I said that about him, I'll deny it." It's true though. Little did I know he was also banging my sister Scarlet on the side.

"Anyway, I loved it," I tell her, then I go deeper. "And I was good at it. Those classes made you think, but in a different way than in school. When I was on that mat, and eventually in that cage, it didn't matter what my last name was or how I scored on a math test. No one was telling me how special I was because of who my dad was. They weren't comparing me to my brothers and sister. I had to earn my place, and it felt fucking fantastic."

"I can't even imagine what that's like," she whispers.

"Which aspect?" I ask because I want to know what makes this woman tick.

"The expectations. I don't remember a time growing up when anyone ever had any expectations of me." As if she realizes what she just said, Maddie clears her throat and straightens. "Okay, so little Hudson liked the classes, but how did that translate to this career?"

"Little Hudson," I laugh. This woman is going to be the death of me. "Dad hated that I did it. He hated that I was fighting. He couldn't understand it. But he never got in my way. Even though I'm pretty sure he wished he could. He sent me to train in Brazil the summer after my senior year in high school, and it was incredible. Watching those men. Their work ethic. Their skills. Their love of the sport. That's when I knew that was what I was going to do. And when I came home, he stopped trying to talk me out of it."

We pull into my driveway and wait for the garage to open. "I'm telling you, Mads, there's just something about being in that cage. Once you step foot on those mats, nothing else matters. Not your name or how much money is in your pocket. Not the color of your skin or where you're from. It's about how much time you've put in. How hard you worked. You decide who you want to be, and ultimately whether you're going to win the fight."

Maddie and I both get out of the car and walk into the house. "How exactly do you decide you're going to win the fight? Wouldn't both of you think that going into the cage?" She bends down and takes the hospital socks off her feet, giving me an incredible view of her delectable ass.

Fuck me . . . I'm going to hell.

My hands itch to touch.

To taste. To take.

But I don't.

No matter how fucking badly I want to.

"Hudson?" Oh right. She asked a question.

"I work harder every day, not just for the six weeks leading up to the fight. I will always work harder. I will always be in control." I follow her like a damn puppy dog when she walks into the kitchen and tosses her dirty socks into my trash can.

She washes her hands, then turns to face me. "Hud, can I use your shower? I feel gross."

"One question first, sunshine." She lifts her stubborn chin higher and waits. "Why did you come home with me tonight?"

When Maddie doesn't answer, I clarify, "Was it really just to avoid your brother?"

The room is silent for one long beat.

Then another before Maddie moves in front of me.

Slowly . . . so fucking slowly, she reaches up and runs her thumb along my jaw.

I'm a strong man, but the strength I have in the cage doesn't compare to the strength I need right now to control my need to touch this woman. But this show is hers. She's in control, and I'll move when she's ready.

But I don't think that's now.

Not yet.

She drops her hand to the front of my hoodie and hooks her fingers inside my pocket, keeping her eyes locked on mine. "No, Hudson." Maddie's top teeth dig into her pouty lower lip. "It wasn't."

I slowly run my hands up her arms, waiting to see if she flinches or backs away before I gather her face in my hands. "Tell me to stop, Madison."

"Don't stop," she pleads, and I don't have to be told twice.

I take it slow, going against every instinct I have but unsure of what Maddie needs, and lower my lips to hers as her eyes drift shut. Softly at first. Testing. Teasing. Making sure she's okay.

I don't want to scare this beautiful woman in my arms.

She tugs at my sweatshirt, pulling me closer, the electricity between us sparking to life as Maddie lifts up on her toes, and the tension that's been building finally detonates. I may have only waited three years for this woman... for *this kiss*, but I kiss her with the need of a hundred years.

I slide my hand to the side of her neck and tangle my fingers in her soft hair, while my thumb presses against her wildly thrumming pulse.

She sighs one of her sexy sighs, and the sound washes over me as my brain starts working through all the ways I want to make this woman sigh. Want to make her fucking scream.

I part her lips with mine and slide my tongue inside her hot mouth, deepening the kiss.

Tasting her.

Wanting more.

Her hands move under my shirt and flatten against the skin of my hips.

And I battle the impulse to lift her in my arms and carry her to my bed.

To bury my tongue in her pussy and make her scream until she soaks my face, then flip her over so I can fuck her from behind with that perfect fucking ass in front of me.

I may want this woman more than I've ever wanted anything in my life, but she needs to stay in control.

We need to take this slow, even if the thought makes me break out in fucking hives.

"Sunshine..." I pull back, and Maddie opens her bright blue eyes as her chest rises and falls in a heavy rhythm. Her lips are bruised and swollen, and her fingers tremble when she lifts them to her mouth, like she can't believe what just happened. "Go shower, Maddie. That was only the first question. You owe me more than one."

Those big blue eyes of hers are heavy-lidded and full of need.

But after a minute, she lowers her hands and fixes my shirt, then finally smiles. "Better make it a good one, King."

I watch her walk out of the room. My eyes stay locked on her until she's out of my sight, then I take ten minutes to ice my knee before I set the alarm and follow her up the stairs.

By the time I make my way to my bedroom, the water has turned off in the bathroom, and steam billows through the open crack in the door. Heating my room and my blood. I step into the closet, stripping out of my shirt and throwing it and my sweats into the laundry basket in the corner of the room. Then I grab a pair of knit pajama bottoms and slide them on.

When I step back into the bedroom, I'm greeted by a sight that makes my cock weep.

Maddie is standing next to my bed. Her flawless skin has a warm pink glow from the shower, and her long hair is damp and piled high on top of her head.

I desperately want to run my tongue up the length of her bare neck until she's squirming. One taste is never going to be enough.

One of the clean Crucible tees from the basket at the foot of my bed is swallowing her, but it fails to hide the bare thighs I want wrapped around me or her hard nipples brushing against the soft fabric. She's fucking perfect, and I'm fucking screwed.

I run my hand over my face and remind myself of Cade's rules.

No drama.

No booze.

No women.

Three days left, and I know, without a doubt I'm breaking at least one tonight.

Maddie

I've been kissed before.

But I never enjoyed it.

I've never been able to get out of my head.

To get comfortable. To feel safe.

It was never anything like *that*.

I was always aware of the hands on my body.

And not in an *oh wow, I want more* kind of way.

Never . . . Until tonight.

Until Hudson.

And now, he's standing in front of me in dark-green pajama bottoms and nothing else. Every inch of the beautifully golden skin of his muscled chest is on display. A gorgeous script stating *Only the good die young* is inked across his collar bones, with an intricate Celtic warrior band forming the top of a sleeve on his arm. Black bands and more detail cover his skin. All of it tells a story I'm desperate to know.

He moves across the room with a confidence few men own, and it's intoxicating. Hud hits a button on the fireplace, and the flames crackle to life as he drops down into one of the two chairs in front of it. "Okay, Madison. Your turn." He pats the seat next to him, and I pad across the room, my toes sinking into the plush, cream carpeting.

"Aren't you supposed to be in bed, King? You've got training tomorrow." I smile, knowing my diversion tactic isn't going to work. But it's worth a try.

He ignores my attempt to stall. "We're not starting tomorrow until ten. I've got time." His eyes lock on my bare legs when I take the seat next to him and rest my feet on the gray ottoman in front of us. They come to a stop where his big shirt hits the top of my thighs, and his gaze burns my skin with want staring back at me.

"Fine. What's your question?" I'm expecting him to ask

why I don't like to be touched. He's done it before, so it would be logical for him to try again. But he doesn't.

"How did you end up in social-media management?" Hud kicks his feet up next to mine, and gently nudges me with them.

A softball question to start with, huh?

I can handle this one, and I'm guessing he knows that. We've always been peripheral friends. We share a circle. But I think we've both paid more attention to each other than either of us has been willing to admit. I think he knows me better than I realized.

And I think I like that.

"Brandon was drafted to play for the Kings my senior year in high school. He petitioned the courts and was granted legal guardianship. I was living with him by the time I graduated and had started handling his social-media accounts for him because he hated doing it. When I started Kroydon Hills University in the fall, I was also doing it for a handful of other players too. It evolved from there, but it wasn't until Daphne started the Start A Revolution Foundation and brought me on board with them and the Revolution that I finally, officially started my own business." I shrug. "Scarlet asked me to freelance for the Kings last year, and the rest is history." I cross one foot over the other and turn his way.

"Then why are you still teaching yoga at the gym?" he pushes.

"Why not? I'm young, and I enjoy it. And not all of us were born with savings accounts big enough to buy small island nations, Kingston." I arch my brow.

"Touché." He nudges my foot again. "I gotcha. Okay, am I allowed to ask why it's just you and Dixon?"

I let my eyes trail over the hard planes of his face, buying myself a minute to get my thoughts together. "That's a long story."

Hudson lounges in the chair. "We've got time."

"This isn't something I really talk about," I admit.

"You don't have to," he offers.

But he's wrong.

I need to share this with him if anything is ever going to happen between us. And I've come to realize, *I do* want something between us. "Brandon and I don't have the same father. Neither of us actually knows who our dads are. But Mom . . . When my mom was sober, she was the best mom in the world. She was beautiful, and she was fun. She used to hold me on her hip and dance with me in the kitchen and do yoga with me in the backyard. But when she wasn't . . . well, I didn't know what it meant back then. I didn't know sober. I just knew she wasn't nice to be around."

I think back to those days. I'm not sure why they're still crystal clear in my mind, but it's like it was yesterday instead of twenty years ago. "Brandon and I shared a room, and even at nine years old, he used to sleep on the floor in front of our bedroom door. She used to have men over all the time. *Uncles*, she'd call them. I didn't understand it back then. He just said he didn't want anyone coming in our room." I figured it out years later, the first time he did it in one of our foster homes. He had a bad feeling, and that night, when the doorknob turned and the door creaked open, it hit Brandon and then shut again.

Hudson's fists white knuckle the arms of the chair.

"I didn't know back then she was an addict." I trail off, remembering how good it used to feel when she smiled down at me.

"Did the state take you and Dix away?" Hud asks as he moves to sit on the ottoman, facing me. He picks up my feet and puts them in his lap as his strong fingers rub my sore arches.

"She died."

Hudson's hands stop, and his eyes find mine. "Mads . . ."

"She died, and she broke me with her." I pull my feet away from him and tuck them under myself. Worry is written all over Hudson's face. He's not sure what to do or what to say, but the hole in the dam that popped open earlier is now a full-blown chasm with raging water pushing against it now.

"Brandon was in third grade, and I was home with Mom because I wasn't starting school until the following fall. I had just turned five. *I thought I was such a big girl.* I had just poured my own cereal." The memory is so clear, it's frightening because I no longer see it through the rose-colored glasses of a five-year-old. I see it for what it was. "When I tried to find her, she was lying on the floor of the bathroom with a needle sticking out of her arm. Her eyes were closed, and I thought she was sleeping . . . but I guess I knew something was wrong because I moved her arm and tucked it around myself, so I could lie down with her."

Hudson sucks in a harsh breath, but I don't look up. I can't. Not now.

"I remember how cold the tile was, and the chemical smell of the bathroom. It was early when I tucked myself against her. After a while, I tried to wake her up. She was supposed to take me to the library, and I wanted to go. But she wouldn't move. Wouldn't open her eyes." It's funny the pieces that are still crystal clear all these years later.

The way her hair tickled my face.

The smudges of mascara giving the illusion of two black eyes.

"I'm not sure how long I was in there before I finally pulled the needle from her arm, thinking she'd wake up then, but she didn't. I think something inside me broke, and that's when I realized she wasn't sleeping. That she wasn't going to come back." I still remember how heavy her body felt against mine. I cried for hours, refusing to move. Tears fill my eyes now, even after all these years, remembering those final moments. "She had aspirated at some point. Then later, after she'd been dead a few hours . . . well, I was lying in my dead mother's arms. In her fluids. And I was scared to move." She was so cold, and so heavy.

"I remember thinking I should have taken the needle out sooner. That maybe that would have helped. By the time Brandon got home from his baseball practice after school, it was five o'clock. I had been with her for something close to nine hours." When I look up at Hud, it's like all the oxygen has been sucked from the room. He looks horrified.

"Brandon and I were placed in our first foster home that night. It was just a temporary placement, but it was the first of so many."

"Sunshine . . ." Hudson stands, then bends down to me. He slides one arm under my legs and the other behind my back, then waits to see what I do.

I guess he's giving me time to tell him no.

To flinch away.

But I don't have any fight left in me.

I wrap my arms around his neck and press my face against his chest as he picks me up and carries me to his bed, like I'm something precious.

"Sleep, Maddie. No one will ever hurt you again."

And with his lips pressed against my head, I close my eyes, believing him.

HUDSON

I've always known I lived a charmed life. But nothing has ever driven that fact home the way Maddie did earlier tonight. I lie awake for hours, watching her sleep. Knowing without a shred of doubt this is where she belongs. Next to me. In my bed. In my arms.

It's funny the way things snapped into focus.

Like somehow, I've always known and only just accepted it.

Is this what it was like for my dad each time he thought he fell in love?

Just as that thought pushes it's way to the forefront of my mind, she tucks herself in closer and presses her lips to my chest.

And suddenly, that's it.

I know I'm done fighting this.

She's it.

As if sensing my warring thoughts, she moves her lips up my body until they're pressed against my jaw. Her arm slides across my chest, and her legs tangle with mine.

She might not be the most comfortable with touching by

day, but she has no problem doing it while she sleeps. When her thumb grazes my nipple and her teeth graze my chin, I pull away.

No way is it going down like this. Maddie half asleep after she just bared her fucking soul is not going to be how we remember our first time together.

"Sunshine," I whisper against her soft skin. "You're driving me crazy, baby."

"Mmm," she hums. "Make me feel something, Hudson," her sleepy voice begs. "I want to feel you. I want you to replace those memories with something else. Something better."

My fingers dig into the warm skin of her waist and flip us over, leaving me hovering above her.

Maddie's heavy eyes flare with desire. She doesn't flinch. There's no pulling away. "I want to replace those memories with you, Hudson." Her nails skim gently over my chest, sending chills racing down my spine. "I want your hands on me."

"Are you sure about this, Madison? Because once we cross this line, there's no going back. You'll be mine, and I won't let you go." I hold myself above her, refusing to let go of her eyes until she answers me.

She reaches up and frames my face as her warm breath fans my jaw. "I'm already yours, Hudson. I think I have been for a while now."

And that's *it*.

That's all I need to hear.

My restraint shatters, and I crash my mouth to hers, swallowing her moan. There's nothing slow or soft about this kiss as I fight myself to stay controlled. We're a clash of teeth and tongues, while my hands skim down her body and Maddie pulls me closer to her, leaving no distance between us and sending every sense into hyperdrive.

I drag my tongue down her graceful neck and smooth my hands up her rib cage, cupping her breast. My calloused thumb traces her nipple, and her back bows off the bed with a sexy little catch in her breath.

"Are you wet for me, Madison?"

She moans when I tug her nipple between my thumb and forefinger. "Yes," she pants.

"Good." I tug at her shirt, ripping it over her head and dropping it to the floor. My eyes trail over her gorgeous body, over her long and toned muscles, covered with creamy, flawless skin I ache to mark. To claim.

My fingers skim over a tiny tattoo at the top of her rib cage I've never seen in any of the skimpy yoga clothes she's worn before. "What's this?" I ask as I bring my lips to the intricate dragonfly inked on her skin.

Something about seeing this ink on her skin drives me fucking insane.

"My dragonfly," she moans as my lips close around her breast.

Whimpering, Maddie's hips lock around me, and she grinds herself against me, looking for relief. "Hud . . ." she begs.

"Tell me what you want," I growl against her skin. "Let me give you what you need." I look down at her, need coursing through my blood, and I run my thumb over her other nipple, loving the way she arches into my palm.

"Make me come, please." She hooks her thigh over my hip and grinds her pussy against my hard cock. Her heat scorches me through her panties while I suck her pale pink nipple into my mouth, tugging it between my teeth.

Maddie's hands slide down my back and over my ass as she lifts her hips against me again and gasps. "What the fuck, Hudson?"

"Madison . . ." I sit up, shocked at the f-bomb she just dropped. "You cursed."

She ignores me as her hand slides around my waist and down the front of my pants until she's wrapping her fingers around my dick through the jersey cotton of my pants. Her big blue eyes grow wide as she bites down on her lip and looks up at me through her thick lashes. "What's this?" she asks quietly with a nervous energy vibrating through her.

I lean back a bit and cover her hand with mine, moving it up and down my shaft. "It's a Jacob's ladder."

Maddie's wild eyes drop down to where are hands are joined as her smile grows. "Really?"

"Yeah, *really*. It's gonna feel so good, baby." I shake my head, not sure if she's going to run screaming or rip my pants off me just to see if I'm telling the truth. Every time I think I know what this woman is thinking, she proves me wrong.

I nip at the soft skin by her tattoo, then slowly work my way down her body. "But don't worry about that yet." My tongue slides over toned abs I've spent years watching as she taught class, then traces lazy circles around her belly button as her stomach quivers before stopping at the edge of her little silk panties.

She smells like the sweetest sin I'll ever commit, and I'm desperate for a taste.

I flatten my tongue and drag it up her sex over the silk, burying my face in her pussy and scraping my teeth against her clit. Her body shakes as she claws at the sheets. "Has anyone ever done this before, Madison?"

"No," she whimpers, and her hips press against my face.

"Good. Because no one else ever will," I growl.

Maddie

Those possessive words are intoxicating.

They caress my skin the same way his strong hands do. And dear God, my entire body lights up like the Fourth of July as he utters them, with his fingers digging into my hips before he rips my panties from my body and buries his tongue in my pussy.

Hudson's strong hands slide to the backs of my thighs as he works my body to heights I didn't know existed. Edging me closer to the brink of an orgasm like nothing I've ever given myself.

I whine when his lips leave my core to trail over my thighs, draping them over his shoulders. Kissing. Licking. Biting. "Hudson," I sob.

Frantic.

For anything.

For everything.

For the oblivion to drag me under.

I'm desperate for him.

"You have such a pretty pussy, sunshine." Cobalt blue eyes hold mine hostage, watching me carefully, cataloging my reactions. A flicker of a smile pulls at his lips as his thick fingers dance circles around my clit. Close, but not enough. Teasing me until I'm writhing beneath him. Begging him. Moaning for him.

He trails his finger down to my drenched sex, circling my entrance and dragging it back up to my clit, nice and lubed. Then he raises his finger to his mouth and sucks. "Fuck, you taste good."

His filthy words pull at something deep and tenuous inside me.

Like a thin thread of spun sugar.

Delicate and fragile and on the verge of shattering.

Hudson pushes his callused finger inside me, curling it against a spot I never knew existed, while he flattens his tongue against my clit and hums. Long, slow strokes of his tongue grow faster. Each one ending with a nip and suck to my clit.

My hands go to his head and tug him closer. Needing more.

I yank his hair, and he groans a long sexy sound that vibrates through my body. "Jesus, baby. You're so fucking tight on my finger." He slips a second one inside me and looks up, his pupils blown wide as I squirm. "You like that, Maddie? Imagine how good it's gonna feel when it's my cock inside you."

Desperation turns to ecstasy as my walls clamp down on his fingers, and I soar. Stars explode behind my eyes, and convulsions rack my body, then he pushes me past any limit I ever thought I'd have. Sucking. Licking. Until he's wrung every last breath from my limp body.

He sits up, and my eyes lock on his before he runs his finger up and down my sex one more time. When I moan, those fingers dip back inside me, then up to my face to trace my lips. "Taste yourself, Madison." He pushes them in my mouth, and I swirl my tongue around the tips, then suck them deep into my throat. My body still hot and needy. Loving what we're doing and ready for more. Eager to please. "That's it," he groans. "Such a good fucking girl."

Hudson's groan of pleasure is the sexiest thing I've ever heard.

Knowing I did that makes me brave, and I trail the tips of my fingers down his chest, over his stacked muscles and cut lines, then underneath the waist band of his pajama bottoms. Ready to return the favor.

But his hand catches mine by the wrist, and in one smooth move, we're turned around on the bed. My back soaks in the warmth against Hudson's chest. One arm is tucked under my head, the other wrapped around me, while his face is buried in my neck. Goosebumps break out over my heated flesh even before his lips press against my skin.

I tilt my head back, disappointed. This feels like heaven, but I want more . . .

As if reading my mind, he whispers against my ear, "Tonight's for you, sunshine. I've got a fight in a few days, and as much as I want to . . . and trust me when I say I really, really want to . . . I can't throw away *all* the rules." He presses his lips to mine, and I relax. "But don't worry. I'm not done with you yet."

I roll over in his arms and wrap myself around him.

Loving the fact that I can.

That this feels right.

"If you have to withhold, then so do I, King. You just said you've got a fight in three days." I kiss him again, slower this time. Cupping his face in my hands. Lightly kissing the outer corner of his lips, his jaw, his forehead. I kiss all the places I've dreamed of kissing on this man. Excitement courses through me that I'm finally able to feel his body relax under my touch. It's a heady feeling. "You need your beauty sleep for your last big day in the gym before the fight." I don't give him a chance to argue and lay my head in the crook of his neck, breathing him in.

Hudson laughs but doesn't argue.

Though I've got a feeling he wants to. His breath evens out, and his arms grow heavy around my body as he drifts off to sleep, leaving me alone with my thoughts on tonight. On this past week. Even the past three years.

Evaluating your life is a nerve-racking thing. Really trying to look at it with a different lens than the one you typically use. A new perspective. It's intimidating. And for me, change is scary. But this change feels like it's for the better. Like it's meant to be.

I'm not sure how much time passes in the silence of the

night, while I'm lost in my thoughts, before I gently press my lips to Hudson's neck and quietly whisper, "I think I was waiting for you to fix me."

His heavy arms tighten around me. "You were never broken, Maddie. And I would have waited forever for you."

MADDIE

"Good morning, sunshine." The bed dips down under Hudson's weight, letting me know he's next to me before his fingers run over my messy hair.

I force my tired eyes open and drag them up his bare chest.

I will never get tired of this view.

"Well, that's good to hear," Hud chuckles, and my face flames with mortification.

Clutching the sheet to my chest, I sit up and hide my face. "I said that out loud, didn't I?"

"Yeah, you did." He presses his lips to the top of my head, and I melt into him, desperate for his touch and not sure how we got here.

"Good morning." My scratchy voice feels forced in the quiet room. "What time is it?"

"Time to get up." He stands and pulls me to my feet, then cups my naked butt, lifting me until I wind my legs around his waist.

"Hudson . . ." I laugh. "What are you doing?"

"Conserving water." He walks us into the bathroom, turns

on the shower, shoves his shorts off, and steps under the spray while I cling to him. "I could get used to this, Maddie."

He runs his nose up the side of my neck, and I arch into him. "Mmm . . . Get used to what?"

"You touching me."

Pulling my head back, I stare into the depths of his eyes and feel like this man is giving me a piece of his soul. And suddenly, I'm desperate for more.

As if he can read my mind, Hudson leans his forehead against mine, groaning, "Three more nights, Maddie."

I kiss the corner of his mouth and squeal when he squeezes my butt, setting me on my feet in front of him. It's the first time I've seen him completely naked, and oh my . . .

"Madison . . . My eyes are up here." He gives me a cocky grin, then squeezes a minty shampoo into his palm and lathers it into my hair.

I can't hold back my contented moan at the sensations and turn around so I can lean my back against him.

Maybe not the best move because now I'm backed up against what feels like a massive, rock-hard, pierced dick. I don't exactly have anything to compare it to, but *wow* . . . I rock my hips back, and Hudson tugs on my hair, warning me, "Madison." This time his voice is clipped, not playful. Strained and sexy. And I find it hard to believe I've done that to him.

I tilt my head back to look at him and get a face full of water. "Do you realize you full-name me when you want me to pay attention?"

"What?" His strong fingers massage my scalp, and I almost forget my point.

Almost . . . "You only call me Madison when you want me to get serious."

He turns my head back around and rinses my hair, leaving me practically purring in his arms. "You're letting me touch you, baby. I'm not sure I take anything more seriously than that."

I shift against him again and smile when his fingers dig into my hips, stopping me. His face dips down, and his voice vibrates along my ear. "The first time I fuck you isn't going to be in a shower, Maddie."

ONCE WE'RE DONE in the shower, we dress quickly and head to the hospital to pick up my car before Hudson makes his way to the gym, which also means we see Daphne and the baby. Hudson holds the hospital door open for me, then laces his fingers through mine as we walk in.

"Let me take you out tonight, sunshine." The words flow so easily from him, but I stop in my tracks.

"What?" I ask, confused. "Like on a date?"

One hand cups my cheek tenderly while he smiles down at me with hungry eyes. "Yeah. Like on a date. I want to take you out, Madison."

"No." I pull my hand out of his and shove it against his hard chest. "The fight is in three days. Take me out on day four."

His smile stretches while his fingers wrap around my wrist. "We're not leaving my bed on day four, sunshine."

Heat pools between my legs at the unspoken promise in those words, and I happily start my own little countdown.

"You're coming to the fight on Saturday, right?" He dips his face lower, crowding me, and a flush rushes to my cheeks.

"Yeah. Chloe and I are going with Cooper and Carys." A swarm of butterflies take flight in my stomach when he presses his lips against my forehead, and I melt into his touch.

"Good. I want to see you there. Coop's tickets are right

behind my family's seats." He's nonchalant about it, like it's the most natural thing for him to say, even though I've never seen Hudson have a date at one of his fights. And I've seen most of them since I started teaching at Crucible.

That thought makes me uneasy as we walk into Daphne's private room to find her sleeping and Max swaying back and forth with Serena in his arms. He takes one look at me, dressed in Hudson's sweats and shakes his head. I'm the epitome of the walk of shame... without the sex. I borrowed a pair of gray sweatpants and one of Hudson's Crucible hoodies to wear today, not wanting to put my black suit back on from yesterday. I have the sweats rolled at my hips, and the hoodie hangs down to mid-thigh, but I don't care. I'm enveloped in the scents of warm cotton and Hudson. It's incredible.

Even if Max Kingston's judgy eyes don't seem thrilled with Hudson.

It's been easy to ignore the reputation I've reminded myself of for years while he's been so different with me. I have a pretty good radar too. And everything inside me screams that there's more to this man than I've given him credit for. But the look in his older brother's eyes tells me exactly how stupid he thinks I am. And that pisses me off.

Hudson ignores the glare Max shoots his way and holds his arms out. "She's perfect, Maximus. Can I hold her?"

Max transfers the tiny little bundle into Hudson's massive arms, and if it's physically possible for my ovaries to spontaneously combust, they would. His big fingers, which had just been all over my body, trace the lines of her perfect little face with such a delicate touch, it makes me ache. *Physically ache.*

"She's incredible, brother." Hudson never looks up to see Max's eyes water, but I don't miss it. This strong man, who owns his world and everything in it, is in awe of his daughter, and I suddenly feel like I don't belong in this room.

Not when my friend is sleeping, and I'm suddenly an intruder on this very personal family moment.

I take a step back toward the door, ready to give them their space.

"Sunshine?" Both men turn toward me.

I point toward my escape just a few feet away. "I thought you might need a few minutes of family time."

"We do," A cocky smile slides onto Hudson's face when he tugs me into him and lowers Serena so I can peek down at her tiny sleeping form tucked into his arms. Max moves behind me, removing my chance at escape, and my emotions war with each other.

I'm intruding on this moment.

This should have been between two brothers.

I don't belong here, even if it's what I wanted.

To be loved. To find someone to love. To be part of something bigger.

THIRTY MINUTES LATER, Serena is sleeping in my arms while Max walks Hudson to his car, so he can get to training on time. And Daphne stares at me, her mouth gaping open.

"I'm sorry . . . what?" She groans as she tries to sit up, her mouth gaping open like a fish trying to breathe.

"We kind of hooked up," I repeat sheepishly, eyeing the door to make sure Max doesn't walk back in while we're having this conversation.

"Mads, what exactly does *kind of hooked up* mean? I don't know if it's exhaustion or just the emotional overload from the past twelve hours, but I'm going to need you to explain this to me in detail." She grimaces when she moves, and my vagina aches in a moment of solidarity with hers.

The door creaks open, and Max walks back in. "I'm

begging you, Maddie. Please. No details." He reaches down and takes Serena from me, then sits down on the bed next to Daphne.

I refuse to laugh at the look of disgust on his face. "I don't kiss and tell, Max."

"That's because you don't kiss, Mads," Daphne snaps. "I want the deets."

I stand up, then kiss Serena's tiny head. "Love you, D. Call me if you need anything."

"Where are you going?" she asks with an indignant pout.

"I'm stopping at Le Désir to see Chloe and Carys, and then I'm going home. I've got work to do." *In more ways than one.*

CARYS AND CHLOE opened their lingerie company a few years ago while they were both still in college. It's grown since then, and their shop on Main Street is now the original flagship of five shops across the country. Chloe likes to say she has a plan for world domination, and I have no doubt those five shops are just the beginning. They've expanded their line over the years, but lingerie is their first love. And their pieces show it.

When I get to their shop, both women are busy with customers, so I peruse the merchandise and start filling my hands with everything I want. I've been addicted to their luxurious confections since they started designing and making them themselves from Chloe's guest room. I love the feel of the lace and silk against my skin. Their lingerie never fails to infuse strength and confidence in me when I get dressed in the mornings. But today, I'm shopping with a different purpose in mind—something more sinful.

Once the last customer leaves, Chloe flips the sign on the

door to *closed*. "You hungry, fashion-disaster?" She's eyeing my clothes with a knowing eye. At least, I had a spare pair of sneakers in my car, so I'm not still wearing last night's heels.

"Busy Bee?" I ask them both, and they nod.

The three of us walk across the street to the Busy Bee Café and take our usual booth, with the two of them on one side and me—minus Daphne, my partner in crime—on the other.

I pull my phone from my purse, ready to take notes. "Okay, are you ready to talk about the social media for the fashion show?"

Carys and Chloe look at each other and laugh. Chloe reaches across the table and swipes the phone from my hands. "That's a fuck no, Mads."

"Spill it, sister," Carys agrees before our waitress places glasses of water in front of us and takes our order.

Once she leaves, all eyes are back on me. "Fine. I'll tell you everything."

By the time I've filled my friends in on most of what happened last night—most, but not everything, because there are some things I shared with Hudson that I've never shared with anyone else—they're completely stunned.

"Holy shit, Mads." Chloe sits back against the booth with a french fry frozen midway to her mouth, while Carys sits next to her with a self-satisfied grin.

I kick Carys under the table. "What are you thinking?" I ask her.

"I think I've been telling Cooper for years that I thought there was something between you and Hudson Kingston, and he always told me I was crazy." She grabs Chloe's fry and pops it into her mouth. "Look who's crazy now."

Chloe elbows Carys for stealing the greasy fry. "Wait . . . Are you saying Mads is crazy, or is Cooper the crazy one? Because he did marry you, after all."

"Hello?" I pluck a tomato from my salad and throw it between them. "Do you think this is nuts? Because I feel like the idea of it should have me so much more scared than I actually am. I'm not sure if I'm being naive or just plain stupid."

"You're not either of those things, Maddie. If your gut is telling you to go for it, then go for it. Just be careful and keep your eyes open." Carys steals another fry from Chloe's plate and dips it into her chocolate shake.

"That is so gross." Chloe pushes her plate in front of Carys, her face pinching tight in disgust at the mixing of food before she turns back to me. "Don't listen to her. Have fun. See where it goes. If nothing else, I bet Hudson Kingston will make it so good for you, Mads."

I realize quickly I don't like either of them talking about him like this, especially when they snicker. "What?"

"Oh, Mads. You should see your face," Carys points at me. "Don't listen to either one of us. Do what feels right to you. Only you get to decide that. But I'd make sure you've got some killer lingerie for Saturday night."

"The white with blue lace?" Chloe asks Carys before they both smile. "Let's get the check. We need to get you fitted."

When I leave the shop a little later, it's with the most gorgeous lingerie I've ever seen in my life and a little extra pep in my step. I love my friends.

HUDSON

Final cut day fucking sucks.

I don't let myself get too out of control between fights anymore because cutting the weight is awful. I'd rather eat dogshit than do a twenty-pound weight cut again. Been there, done that. Won the fight. But none of that means I want to repeat that soul-crushing process, so I try to make sure I have less than that to cut during camp.

Most of it is water weight.

We all cut it, weigh in, and then start the process of rehydrating after the press junket ends.

That's tomorrow. Two more nights before I defend my title against Maniac McGuire, and when I walk into Cade's office, Spider Reynolds is taunting me again. This time on a national sports vlog. "What the fuck?"

Cade looks up, tells me to shut the door, then turns the TV up.

Spider's been spouting off to anyone who'll listen that this fight's a joke.

That McGuire has no chance.

That it's a soft fight because I'm scared to face a real fighter.

That my last name bought my title.

Like I haven't spent the past five years fighting the best in this sport.

The scumbag just wants his shot. But he doesn't want to earn it.

"How many times am I going to have to ignore this shit?" I grunt. "I've got no problem doing it. But at some point, I'm going to destroy this asshole."

Cade turns the TV off, then spins back around to me. "Ignore him. He's nothing. He's a hack, looking for an easy way up. And he's not getting it from you. Two more days, King. Don't split your focus." He eyes me carefully, and I read between the lines.

"I'm not breaking any rules, Saint."

"That's up for interpretation," he argues, but there's no heat behind his words. "Go home. I'm staying late tonight. I'll make sure Maddie and Imogen get out of here."

"Any word from the cops?" Kroydon Hills isn't a huge town. We're on the outskirts of Philly and have our own police force. The crime level is pretty damn low, considering.

I don't understand why the hell this investigation is taking so long.

"Nah. Not yet. Sam sent over someone who upgraded the security though, so we should be good. Either way, I'm working on hiring a night manager, so none of the girls have to be here alone when they're closing. One of the guys is staying with Imogen tonight." He closes his laptop and rises from his chair. "Get out of here, King. Go home. Rest. I'll see you in the morning."

When we step into the hall, my niece flies at me. She wraps her arms around my shoulders and her gangly legs around my waist. "Uncle Huddy," Brynlee squeals.

"Hey, Brynnie. What's shakin'?" I blow a raspberry on her cheek and squeeze.

"Hey, munchkin. What about me?" Cade reaches for his daughter, who rolls her eyes like a teenager.

"I saw you this morning, Daddy. I haven't seen Uncle Huddy in a long time."

Jesus, this kid has me wrapped around her little finger.

"Missed you too, sweets." I bounce her on my hip. "Where's your mom?"

Brynlee points toward the front desk where Scarlet and Imogen are talking.

"How was London?" I ask her about her trip to watch the Kings play, and her whole face lights up.

"We saw a real castle last week. And it was guarded by these men in funny hats who weren't allowed to talk." She looks at me with wide eyes, her blonde curls bouncing around her animated little face. "Like, at all," she gasps.

"The horror," I dramatically gasp back, then tickle her sides until her giggling fills the gym.

Her little brother, Killian, toddles over and grabs my sweats. I bend down and pick him up, then shift Brynn so they're each on a hip. "Hey, killer." Killian yawns in my face, then I lean over and kiss Scarlet's cheek. "Hey, sis."

"Mommy's being mean. She won't let me see you fight this weekend. I tried telling her I see you fight here all the time, but it didn't work."

"Brynlee," Scarlet sighs. "We've been over this. You're too young."

Brynn pushes to be let down, then plants her feet on the ground and dramatically slams her hands on her hips. Imogen stifles a laugh behind me. "I'm almost six years old, Mom."

I swear it's the tone that does it.

Six going on sixteen, maybe.

Scarlet shakes her head. "The answer is no."

"We're going to grab dinner, Hudson. Why don't you join us?" Scarlet looks hopeful, like she thinks I'd go out to dinner the night before weigh-ins.

Cade wraps his arm around my sister and directs her toward the door. "He's got weigh-ins and the press tomorrow and then a fight Saturday, duchess. Let the man do what he's gotta do tonight. He can enjoy everything else after the fight on Saturday."

Scarlet's pout resembles the face Brynlee made when she didn't get her way. "Fine. But you better be at the Kings game Sunday. It's home at one."

She stands there, waiting for me with an expectant glare.

"Scar . . . I've been in training for six weeks. I'm not getting out of bed on Sunday." She doesn't need to know I don't plan on being alone.

"Hudson Thaddeus Kingston."

Killian buries his head against my chest, like he thinks he's the one in trouble, and Brynlee oohhhs . . . "She middle-named you, Uncle Huddy. Mommy only middle-names us when we're in trouble."

Her innocent statement reminds me of Maddie, and a smile pulls at my lips.

Would she want to go with me to a Kings game?

She's usually there watching her brother anyway.

Would she sit with my family? On my arm?

"Fine," I agree. "I'll be there."

As if reading my mind, she asks, "Alone?"

Cade takes Killian from me, then wraps his arm around his wife's shoulders. "If anyone in the goddamn gym could just wait two more days before complicating my fighter's life, it would be a miracle."

"Daddy cursed. That's a dollar for the swear jar." Brynlee's hands go back to her hips, and I laugh again.

"That swear jar is gonna put these kids through college," Cade mumbles.

"Sure. That's what's gonna do it." I ignore the pissed-off look on his face and say goodbye to my sister's family and wonder, for one of the first times ever, if that's actually in the cards for me.

Maddie

Hudson and Imogen are both waiting for me at the front desk once my class ends. I walk my students to the door, like always, then lock it behind me and turn to face these two goofballs, who laugh simultaneously at whatever they're watching on Gen's phone.

They look up as I walk toward them, and Gen pops up from her seat. "Last night of cleaning the mats. Woo hoo!"

Really? Has it only been a week?

My eyes find Hudson's as if tethered to him by an invisible string.

It's crazy how much can change in seven days.

"Is someone scheduled to close with you tonight, Imogen?" I thought I saw one of the guys on the updated schedule in the office earlier.

"Yup. I'm good. You two crazy kids get out of here." She moves to the mats with the cleaner in her hand, leaving Hudson and me alone at the desk.

"I've got to grab my stuff from the locker room. Thanks for waiting for me." I lower my voice. "You didn't have to."

His big palm runs over the back of my head before pulling on a braid. "I wanted to. We didn't get a chance to talk today."

Hudson follows me to the locker room, filling me in on cut day.

"That sounds awful, King." I pull my bag out and slip my sweats on over my leggings, then turn around. Like a switch flipped, Hudson's on me. His arms cage me in against the locker on either side of my face, and his breath tickles the sensitive skin under my ear. He's everywhere but not physically touching me anywhere.

I ball my hands into fists at my sides.

Wanting to yank him close.

But not wanting to break the rules.

Not now.

"Hudson..."

His nose trails up my neck, just a whisper of a hot breath away from my skin. Burning me from the lack of touch. "Two more nights, baby."

God. Why does that sound like the most sinful promise ever made?

I close my eyes and try to slow my racing heart. "Two more nights. You better not get hurt Saturday, King."

He takes a forced step back and reaches for my bag. "Don't jinx me, woman."

He walks me to my car and opens my door. "I'm going to follow you home."

"No. You're not. I can drive myself home. You need to go home, eat, and rest. Please. You said it yourself. Two more days. Don't mess it up now, when you're so close." I lean up on my toes and brush my lips over his cheek. "Call me tomorrow when it's over?"

Hudson's thumb strokes my cheekbone. "Yeah. I'll see you tomorrow, sunshine." He stands there, watching me until I pull out of the parking lot. And for a reason I'm not 100 percent ready to overanalyze yet, there's a tug on my heart when I leave him.

That tug is gone when I walk into the house a few

minutes later and run right into Brandon. He steadies me with his hands on my shoulders. "Hey, slow down."

"Sorry," I mumble as I try to sidestep him.

I've managed to avoid him since the other night. Not an easy thing to do when you're the only two people in the house. But if you can't make it work, you're not trying hard enough.

"Mads, come on . . . You can't keep ignoring me." Brandon's voice holds an air of irritation in it.

"Pretty sure I can." I keep moving toward the stairs until he dashes in front of me, blocking the bottom step.

"Madison, stop. I'm sorry I upset you." Screw him for being so good at choosing his words.

"Brandon . . . you're not sorry for your actions. You're just sorry that I'm mad. That's not enough." I shove past him, steam practically raging out of my ears. "You're not my father. We didn't have them. You don't get to tell me what to do. I don't care how much older than me you are."

He follows me into my room. The rage building between us is a living, breathing thing. "You're kidding me, right? I've taken care of you your entire life. I'm not your father. I was better than him because I'm still here. I've never let anyone hurt you."

I spin around, the fury simmering just beneath my skin. "And I'd trust you with my life. But I'm an adult, Brandon. You can't treat me like a child."

"But it's my job," he yells. "It's always been my job, Maddie. And I don't know how to stop."

"You've got to take a step back, big brother. I love you. I appreciate you and everything you've done for me. But you've got to let me make my own decisions and live my own life. You can't go talk to my boss." I feel the tips of my nails digging into my palms from fisting them too tightly. "You don't get to unilaterally make decisions for me. You've got to figure out your own life and stop getting stuck in mine." The words are out of my mouth before I can think them through, and I immediately wish I could pull them back.

The pain shining in his eyes hurts my heart.

"Brandon . . . I didn't—"

"No." He steps back, his eyes blazing. "I need to get my own life straight before I can tell you how to live yours." He walks out of my room and slams the door so hard, it bounces off the hinges.

Great.

HUDSON

I go home to my empty house, eat a light dinner, ice my damn knee, and watch ESPN. All that takes about an hour—maybe less—before I realize this isn't where I want to be. This house I spent close to a year fixing up. The one I painstakingly refinished so every inch would be exactly what I wanted... This house feels empty. It feels cold.

How the hell can things change so quickly?

So completely?

I don't want to be here. I want to be *there*. With her.

I'm balancing on a tightrope strung together by rules.

Rules I know I can't break. *Won't break.*

But the beauty of rope is you can bend it to your will and shape it to your needs.

And I need to be next to her.

That's how I find myself sitting in Maddie's driveway, staring at her darkened window and thinking about how I want to feel her body wrapped in my arms, when a fist bangs against my hood.

Fuck.

I open the door and come face-to-face with a pissed-off Brandon Dixon on the other side. "Sorry, man. I was just..."

Yeah. I'm not sure what I was *just* doing, but I'm pretty sure I'm not telling him.

"Jesus Christ, Kingston." He cups his hands around his mouth and blows on them. "I'm freezing my fucking balls off out here. Come inside or go home. Cause right now, you look like a desperate stalker. And I don't let stalkers near my sister."

Without overthinking it, I grab my bag from the passenger seat and follow him into his house.

Cinder greets me once the door closes, winding her way between my legs and swishing her white-tipped tail behind her. The light of the TV is the only thing illuminating the first floor of the darkened house. "Is Maddie awake?"

Something unreadable flashes across Dixon's face. I don't know him well enough to know if it's anger or hurt. But something is bothering him. "I don't know. She's not talking to me."

"Oh shit. I've got sisters. I know what that's like." Scarlet can hold a grudge longer than any of my siblings, but Lenny's not too far behind.

"Yeah well, I don't. Maddie's never been mad at me before." He sits down on the couch and rests his elbows on his knees, not looking at me. "I didn't do anything differently, but this time, she lost her mind. She's furious. And that's not like my sister."

This should be weird, right? Maddie's brother talking to me, her new man, about her.

Wait . . . I don't like that. I'm not her *new man* because there wasn't an *old man*.

I'm her *only* fucking man.

Damn, this woman brings out every overprotective, asshole alpha instinct I have.

"Listen, you know Maddie in a way I never will, so take this with a grain of salt, if you want. But I think you might need to keep in mind that you've helped your sister become this incredible, strong, confident woman. She's put me in my place with ease and a smile more than once over the years. You might need to give her a little room to breathe." Okay. That wasn't too bad.

Dixon drags his hand down his face, then grabs a beer from the side table. "Want one?" he asks, and I shake my head no. "I swear to God, I'm never having kids. I thought this would be easier once Maddie was grown. But it's not. It just keeps getting harder, and I have no clue what the hell I'm doing. I can't deal with this shit."

I guess I shouldn't tell him the thought of his sister pregnant with my baby doesn't even remotely scare me. Instead, a rush of need surges through me with that thought. But I should probably tell her that, not him. And that conversation isn't happening tonight.

After an awkward moment, I point toward the stairs. "I'm just gonna . . . yeah." I take two steps before Dixon interrupts me.

"Don't fuck this up, Kingston. I never thought I'd like anybody who's interested in Maddie. You're still not good enough for her, but she could do worse."

"Thanks, man." Maybe if I didn't have sisters, I'd think this guy was an asshole. But I know what it's like to just want them to be protected, even though I know they can take care of themselves.

I turn back and make my way up the stairs.

Maddie's door is already cracked open when I brush my knuckles against it gently.

Well, shit.

I hadn't thought about what I'd do if she didn't answer.

No turning back now.

Quietly, I open her door and let myself in her room, then stand there, staring at my sunshine. Her golden hair is spread out on her pillow like a halo framing her gorgeous face. The moonlight streaming in through the windows illuminates long black lashes lying against her cheeks. And her hands are tucked up under her head while the rest of her is buried under a mountain of blankets.

She's an angel, and I'm the lucky son of a bitch she's trusted with her heart.

At least, I hope she does.

I kick off my sneakers, pull my shirt over my head, and climb into bed.

As if sensing me, she scoots back, and I wrap my arms around her, dragging her against my chest. She wiggles into me, adjusting herself to be my little spoon, then wraps both of her arms around mine.

That's it. That's all it takes for this woman to be safe in my arms. No hesitation. No resistance. She's so damn welcoming when she's sleeping, and I finally relax.

"Mmm... Hudson?" her sleepy voice murmurs.

I press my lips to the top of her head. "Yeah, baby. It's me. Go back to sleep."

"What are you doing here?" Maddie rolls over to face me, then kisses my chest before she molds herself to me.

"Couldn't sleep without you." Might as well lay it out there.

"Couldn't or wouldn't?" She yawns, her eyes still closed.

"Doesn't matter. Just needed to be here, Mads."

She weaves her legs through mine and presses her lips to my neck. "You say the sweetest things." Her breathing evens out within seconds, and nothing else is said.

And as I drift off, I realize this is the most at peace I've been in years.

BEING the reigning champion meant one thing when it came to contract negotiations for this fight. I was able to insist it be in Philly. I've won my title and defended it in Las Vegas, New York City, Atlantic City, and Seattle. It was time my city got some love. It was also convenient as hell.

We're at the convention center for weigh-ins today and for the fight tomorrow.

Once they announce each of us and do the ceremonial weigh-ins—as if they didn't just do the official ones thirty minutes ago backstage—we pose for pictures and some good-natured shit-talking. Then Maniac and I take seats at the long table with our coaches and prepare for questions from the press.

They throw out softballs.

What do you think of your opponent?

How was your camp?

When they ask what my plan for after the fight is, I laugh. No need for them to know I plan on spending twenty-four hours in bed worshipping Madison Dixon. Instead, I tell them, I'm going to Disney World.

We're all laughing when a voice calls out from the back of the crowd. "When are you gonna fight a real fight, Kingston? You like callin' yourself *King*. You like sittin' in that ivory tower. But you ain't earned shit, man."

"Is that a challenge, Reynolds?" the announcer asks.

Cade stands so I won't. "Get out of here, Reynolds, before I throw you out of here the way I threw you out of my gym."

A resounding *ohhh* is heard bubbling through the crowd. And this asshole's cheeks burn bright red. His face gives away every move he's going to make before he moves. It always has. He's never been a skilled fighter, just a lucky one.

And when he charges the stage and has to be held back by security, no one in the room is surprised.

"You gonna let that hot little piece of ass protect you again this time, King?" he sneers, and I see red.

I stand, and Cade's hand presses down against my shoulder, reminding me not to throw away what I've been working toward. "Earn the fight, motherfucker. Earn the fucking fight, and I already told you, I'll beat you anywhere. Anytime. Stop trying to get everyone to listen to your bullshit and earn the fucking fight," I demand. But it's too late. The guards are escorting him out while the questions get thrown at me all at once.

They're all about Maddie.

Who is she?

Does she have a name?

Is she my girlfriend?

Did I steal her from Spider?

They get more ridiculous with each question, and I refuse to answer any of them.

Cade pushes me from the stage, telling the MC I'm done for the day.

I head to the warm-up room that's already been set up for tomorrow's event and dress while Cade yells into his phone at Imogen. "Control the damn story, Gen. This is bullshit. He's trying to throw Hud off his game."

My blood boils the longer I stand in this room and listen to Cade go into management mode.

"Fix it," he tells her again, then pockets his phone. "Fuck, man. I fucking told you no women. You don't need to be dealing with this shit right now. I need your head clear. I need you focused." He puts both hands on my shoulders and stares at me, like that's gonna zen me out or some shit.

News flash—it's not.

"I swear to God, I'm gonna kill that fucker," I growl, the words vibrating from my chest.

"Focus, King." He squeezes my shoulders. "Focus on tomorrow. You can fight that pencil-dicked shit any time you want. Fuck." He looks up to the ceiling. "I'll even let him back in Crucible, if that's what you want, just so you can kick his undiscipline, lazy ass all over my mats. I'll fucking do it myself if you don't want to. But we're not worrying about him right now. We're focusing on McGuire. We're focusing on tomorrow. We're focusing on the win."

When I grind my teeth and refuse to answer him, he asks again, "We good?"

"Yeah, Saint. We're good."

Neither of us believe it.

But it'll have to do for now.

I'll be better when I can work it out in the cage tomorrow.

MADDIE

How were weigh-ins?

HUDSON

204 pounds of solid muscle.

MADDIE

Maybe you should add a little yoga into your workout routine. Sounds like you're getting kinda chunky, King.

HUDSON

Did you just call me fat, woman?

MADDIE

I did no such thing.

HUDSON

Be careful, Mads. No bruising my fragile ego the day before a fight.

MADDIE

Pretty sure your fragile ego is rock solid and intact.

HUDSON

It might need a little help, sunshine.

MADDIE

Okay. How about this. Wanna know a secret?

HUDSON

Did Daphne finally figure out that Maximus likes dressing up in women's clothes?

MADDIE

You're terrible, and he does not.

HUDSON

Come on. Tell me your secret.

MADDIE

I liked waking up with you today.

HUDSON

You're going to like going to bed with me tomorrow even more.

MADDIE

Should I leave the door unlocked tonight?

HUDSON

What time are you done working tonight?

MADDIE

My last meeting should be over by six.

HUDSON

How about I bring dinner to you?

CAGED

MADDIE

You sure? I can come to your house.

HUDSON

Nah. Let me come there. And text me what Dixon wants to eat.

MADDIE

He and I aren't really talking.

HUDSON

Cut him a break, Mads. We're guys. We don't know how to express ourselves when we're trying to protect our sisters. I fucked up with Scarlet and Cade a few years ago.

MADDIE

Why'd she forgive you?

HUDSON

I groveled.

MADDIE

He hasn't groveled.

HUDSON

I talked to him last night. He feels like shit.

MADDIE

He should. He was a jerk.

HUDSON

We're men. We're going to mess up.

MADDIE

Then I guess you better get good at groveling.

I GO in search of my brother late Friday afternoon, but he's not in any of his usual places. The family room is empty, the

TV turned off. No sign of life in the kitchen, not even the gym in the basement. I know he's home from practice. I heard him come in while I was on a call with a client earlier. But he's been quiet since.

We've both been quiet this week.

It's not until Cinder paces in front of the sliding-glass doors that I catch sight of him sitting on the back deck. A light dusting of snow is falling, covering his black sweater, and Brandon is sitting there in the middle of it, sipping something in a rocks glass.

He doesn't look up when I step outside.

Not even when I take the glass from him and sip.

The fiery liquid burns my throat, warming me from the inside out. "We need to buy a Christmas tree, not drink something that tastes like one."

"It's gin, Mads." He takes the glass back and looks out over the backyard. "Did you ever think we'd be here? After all those years in all those foster homes . . . I never actually believed we'd make it out."

"Brandon . . ." Any lingering anger I may have been holding onto disappears with the vulnerability in his admission.

"I mean, I knew we had to. I knew I had to get you out of there. But I was so fucking scared I couldn't. I just needed a scholarship. I knew that was our golden ticket. That was our first chance at freedom. At safety. But that meant I had to leave you alone for the first time." He finishes his gin and slams it a little too hard against the table. "I had to do it, Maddie. I had to take that chance so we could be safe."

I stand there in shock.

This isn't something we talk about. *Ever.*

"Brandon, would you *please* look at me?" When his nearly obsidian eyes finally lift, there's so much pain barely contained within their depths, it threatens to bring me to my knees. "You've always been my protector. You've always kept me safe. And I know you've done it at your own expense."

I sit down next to him on the chilly, wet chair and knock my knee against his. "It's always been us against the world, and I think we've done a pretty good job. I held my own while you were gone. And it's not like you didn't stop by every night after practice." I try to lighten the mood by giggling at the memory. "You smelled awful half the time. Like you brought every dirty gym sock in existence home with you." When he doesn't even crack a smile, I get serious. "You've always been there. But it's time. I need you to start letting me face a little more of it on my own."

"Maddie, you have no idea what the thought of you getting hurt did to me." He wraps an arm around my shoulder, and I rest my head against his. "I know you're a strong woman, but it's always been my job to take care of you. To not find out what happened until after I got home from London made me feel completely helpless, and I haven't felt that way since we were kids."

"But that's the thing. We're not kids anymore. You slayed all the monsters, Brandon." An errant tear trails down my cheek before I have a chance to blink it back. "And now you've got to trust that I can do that myself."

"Will you talk to me again if I say I'm working on it?"

A snowflake gets caught on my lashes, and a chill skirts down my spine. "I'll talk to you again if we can go inside where there's heat."

"Mads . . ." Brandon pulls me to my feet. "Have you ever thought about talking to someone about everything?"

My stomach drops, and a ball of nerves clogs my throat, threatening to choke me. "Like a therapist?"

Brandon nods.

"I guess I've thought about it. But it's not something I've ever actively looked into." Maybe I should. Maybe it would help. We walk into the warm house, and I shake the tiny snowflakes from my hair.

"I made an appointment to talk to someone next week."

I look at my brother, my protector. Really look at him. This man who's been keeping me safe since before I even knew what he was doing, and I realize it's my turn to keep *him* safe.

I lace my fingers through his and squeeze. "Can I go with you?"

MADDIE

"Are you already there?" I ask Hudson whose handsome face is smiling back at me through FaceTime.

"Yeah. We got here a while ago. I've got to start stretching soon." He lowers his voice and licks his lips. "You got your bag packed?"

Apparently, he wasn't quiet enough because Cade comes into view, scowling. "Off the phone, King. Get your head in the fight." He smacks the back of Hudson's head, and I smother a laugh.

"I'll see you after," I whisper, not liking the idea that everyone can hear us.

His image bounces as he walks away from his team bustling around the room. "Text Coop when you get here. I want to see you before the fight."

I bite down on my bottom lip with heady anticipation. "Are you sure?"

My bedroom door swings open, and Carys and Chloe walk in with Le Désir bags in their hands. "Is that him?"

Chloe asks, sticking her face in front of my phone. "Don't suck tonight, Kingston."

"Hang up the fucking phone, King," Cade yells, and Hudson laughs.

"He's never going to get used to the fact that I thrive in chaos. I'll see you soon, sunshine." Hudson ends the call, and I toss my phone on my bed.

"Holy shit. Look at your face," Carys gasps as I feel my flush growing. "You're so red."

"Mads, red is not your color." Chloe hands me a bag. "But lucky for you, blue and gold definitely are."

"What are you talking about?" I peek into the bag filled with boxes. "What did you two do?"

Carys flops down on my bed, already dressed and ready for tonight's fight. "Nothing."

Chloe simultaneously replies, "Everything. Now look at the goodies we've brought you."

I pull out three separate boxes, all wrapped in purple ribbon with the black-foiled Le Désir labels glinting in the light. Once I open the first one, my fingers trace the royal-blue silk and gold lace tucked between tissue paper. It's soft and decadent against my skin, and they're the same color as the shirt Hudson wears when he walks into the cage for each fight.

I hold the bra and panties up, dangling them from the tips of my fingers and flush. "These are beautiful."

Carys opens the second box and pulls out a gorgeous blue silk corset. "We thought you might want to wear this tonight. You know . . . to the fight."

I hold it in front of myself and look in the mirror. It'll show a little more skin than I typically go for if I'm not in the gym, but I can't ignore the tingles I get at the thought of Hud seeing me in this top. "What would I pair something like this with?"

"Tight, dark jeans and sky-high heels," Carys tells me with a flair. "They need to hug your ass, Mads."

Chloe snags the panties from my hands and flips them around to show off the high-cut lace on the back side. "That man has a thing for your ass, Mads. So, Brazilian panties all the way. Just enough to cover. To tempt and tease."

"How would you know what he has a thing for?" I question, and she laughs at me.

"Because I've watched him watching you teach your class. It's obvious to anyone who's not you. Besides . . . you've got a great ass. I'd do you."

"Aww . . . If I swung that way, I'd totally be down." I open the other boxes and find two more sets of lingerie and two nighties. "It's one night, guys."

"It's the first night, Mads, not the only one." Carys grabs my overnight bag from the floor and adds the additional lingerie to it. "Now, go get dressed. I told Cooper we'd be there in thirty minutes."

CARYS LIED. We don't make it to the convention center in thirty minutes. By the time we're escorted to our seats, it's closer to an hour later, and Coop has been blowing up Carys's phone for the past ten minutes.

Hudson's family is seated already, spanning the row in front of us and talking among themselves as the three of us move to take our seats. But before we have a chance to sit down, Cooper appears and kisses his wife.

"So much for half an hour, babe," he kids. Coop's dressed in a royal-blue Crucible shirt, which I'm assuming matches the rest of Hudson's team and everyone representing our gym family. Supporting Hudson.

He reaches out for my hand. "Hudson wants to see you before the fight starts, Maddie."

I slide out of the row of seats and let Cooper guide me through the packed house of spectators, back down the roped-off corridor, and past the security guards who are half the size of the men they're protecting. Undercard fights have been happening for hours already, crowding the halls long before Hudson and his team got here.

Coop knocks on a heavy door before Imogen opens it and steps aside, and a wave of nervous energy washes over me.

Cade's glare is the first thing I see, and it grows with each step I take deeper into the crowded room. But I block him out and move around the space until I find Hudson at the very back, sitting on what looks like a padded massage table. His dark shorts fit snug over his muscled quads, and that shirt I knew I'd be matching stretches tightly over his powerful chest, highlighting every hard ridge and rippling muscle. His golden skin is glowing under the light, and my goodness . . . Is it possible to spontaneously go up in flames? Because this man lights a fire in me. He makes me feel things I've never felt before and want things I didn't think I ever would. Heat builds slowly until I can feel it singeing the strands of my hair, while I stand in this chaotic, testosterone-filled room, anticipating being alone with him later. Imagining myself *finally* licking every line of his ink tonight.

A league official is watching someone tape Hudson's hands before he signs his initials on Hud's knuckles, then leaves the room.

Cade whistles, getting everyone's attention. "Okay, let's focus, King."

Hudson's dark eyes meet mine and hold me in place as excitement moves down my skin. "Can everyone give us the room for a minute?" The statement is worded like a question, but the commanding voice is demanding, not asking.

The tension hangs so thick, the weight of it sits heavy in the air. And Hudson's eyes never leave mine.

Nobody responds. They simply begin to filter out of the room, but I stay put, knowing deep down I'm who he wants in here.

Cade, however, doesn't move either.

"King—" Cade starts, but Hudson doesn't give him the chance to finish.

"Just give us a minute, coach." His tone is clipped.

Cade's expression is tight when he shuts the door behind himself, leaving us alone.

"Come here, sunshine." Hudson's velvety voice wraps around me and tugs. His hungry eyes warm my skin as I walk into his outstretched arms. I cup the back of his head in my hands and lean my forehead against his, breathing him in.

We connect in the stillness, absorbing the magnitude of the moment.

The energy in the room has a static charge, and *this* feels important.

Being here before *this* fight.

Being in his arms while he silently centers himself.

"You're sitting with my family."

"Yeah, King. The girls and I are right behind your family." I run my fingers through the short hair at the nape of his neck. "Do you need anything?"

"No, baby. You're here, and I'm ready. That's all I need. We'll have to make an appearance at Kingdom afterward, then we'll go home."

With every breath he exhales, I inhale. "You gonna win tonight for me, King?" I tease and scrape my nails lightly against his scalp. "I can be your prize."

"You're gonna be my everything, Madison."

With a soft inhale, I lift my head and drag my shaking thumb over his bottom lip. "Then I guess you better go win this thing."

He doesn't kiss me.

This isn't sexual.

It's so much more.

Two people realizing that *we're* so much more.

"I've got to get back out there," I whisper, knowing my time is running out.

Hudson pulls me closer for a single beat before dropping his hands. "Can you send Cade back in, sunshine?"

"Of course. I'll see you soon." I smile and walk out of the room, coming face-to-face with Cade on the other side of the door. "He's asking for you."

I TAKE my seat behind Hud's brothers, next to Carys and Chloe, and try to control the nervous energy bubbling beneath my skin. "I don't know how I'm supposed to sit here and watch someone hit him," I tell the girls.

Jace Kingston turns around smiling. "You're not. Hudson doesn't take too many hits. These fights don't last long, Maddie." The hot-shot hockey player may not be as tall or broad as his older brother, but that cocky grin and sexy confidence definitely seem to run in the family.

Sawyer smacks the back of Jace's head.

Jace pulls back and glares. "Ow. What the fuck, Huck Finn?"

"Don't jinx him, jackoff." Sawyer grumbles something else, then turns to me. "Ignore him, Maddie. Hudson's got this."

The lights dim and Mason "Maniac" McGuire's intro music is played as he's announced.

My hands begin to shake, while McGuire takes his time walking to the cage, surrounded by his team. Once he steps inside, he seems bigger than before. Scarier than I want him to be.

"I don't know if I can watch this," I whisper over the heavy bass in the dark room before the music changes.

Chills break out over my entire body as the first chords of Avenged Sevenfold's "Hail To The King" are pumped into the arena, and a loud roar is heard from the crowd when Hudson is announced. He owns the room while he walks to the cage, followed by Cade and Cooper with Jax holding his last title belt proudly in the air.

I think I might actually pass out from lack of oxygen. "I can't breathe," I tell Carys before she grips my hand.

His golden skin glistens over every hard-earned dip and muscle when Hudson removes his shirt and flexes, stretching one last time. He jumps high in the air, pulling his knees up to his chest as he goes. Then he bounces on the balls of his feet, the muscles in his thighs bunching and pulling and sweat already glistening on his skin.

Cade grabs both sides of Hud's head and pulls him in, forehead to forehead, telling him something I can't hear and probably don't want to know, before he releases Hudson and moves himself out of the cage.

Both fighters meet in the middle of the cage with the ref standing between them.

The ref goes over the rules, giving them instructions for a fair fight.

They bump fists, and my stomach revolts as they go back to their sides.

The ref signals to start the fight, and both men attack without hesitation or fear.

McGuire punches Hudson in the face, and I close my eyes

and peek through my fingers, like a child watching a horror movie, only this is real life.

They circle each other, getting space and sizing each other up.

The Kingstons are on their feet in front of me, screaming and yelling for their brother.

The girls and I jump to our feet, not wanting to miss anything.

"Oh God, how bad is it that he's been hit already?" I ask no one in particular, then scream as McGuire goes for Hud's legs.

Hudson brings his bad knee up and nails McGuire in the face as the crowd goes insane with a deafening roar.

McGuire falls backward like he's a solid sheet of ice as he hits the mat, and the announcer grabs Hudson's hand and holds it high in the air, declaring him the winner and still reigning world champion by a knockout.

MADDIE

After Hudson showers and changes, we slide into the backseat of a limo, and he pushes a button to lower the divide between us and the driver. "Hey, man. Do you think you could make it take a while to get to the bar?"

My face flames red, and I bury it into Hudson's shoulder.

"Absolutely, sir." The driver closes the divide, and Hudson is on me in a single heartbeat.

"Jesus Christ, Madison." He pulls me onto his lap, and my legs fall open on either side of his thighs as my hands splay flat against the starched cotton dress shirt covering his muscled chest. The adrenaline of the night is bubbling just beneath my skin, excitement and anticipation twining together and rocketing through my veins like a drug.

Rough, calloused fingers trail over my collarbone, then down to trace the top of my plumped-up breasts. "You're in my colors." His hot tongue follows the same trail his fingers just forged, and I shift against the hardness pressing between my legs.

With shaking hands, I unbutton the top few buttons of his shirt and press my lips to the ink on his skin. "Do you like it?" I lick a line of his ink. "The girls made it for me." My lips move up to his ear before I sink my teeth into the lobe and whisper, "Just wait until you see what's underneath it."

He flips me onto my back, and my breath leaves me in a woosh.

Hungry eyes devour me while his fingers dig into my hips. "It's not nice to tease a man, Madison. Especially when that man has been fantasizing about this moment."

I lift my head and capture his lips. "Who said I was teasing, King?"

"I'm not taking your virginity in the back of a limo. But there are other things we can do." His voice holds whispers of a promise I can't wait for him to keep.

"You're right." I kick my heels off and push against his chest until he leans back. "There are. And I want to do them all." Slipping off the leather bench, I kneel on the carpeted floor between Hudson's thighs and pop the button on his jeans.

Hudson bites his lip as one hand sinks into my hair.

The metallic sound of his zipper lowering mixes with our heavy breathing, and I relish the fact that I want to do this. That I'm not scared. That I'm not flinching away from touching or being touched. It's empowering.

His hand doesn't push. It doesn't guide. It's possessive and protective.

He's giving me control.

I look up at him through fluttered lashes and inch down his dark denim and black boxer briefs until his dick juts free, long and thick with metal piercing the bottom. My thumb rubs over two rows of small silver balls, and a shiver runs down the length of him.

The moment I drag my thumb through the pearl of precome glistening at the tip, I suck in a quick breath. And without overthinking it, I press my thumb against my tongue and moan at the salty sweet taste of him.

Hudson groans long and low as his head falls back against the seat, creating such an erotic sight in front of me that I rub my legs together to relieve some of the pressure building in me.

"Hudson." His eyes flash open when I take his other hand in mine and place it on my face. "I want your hands on me. I want you to tell me what you like. Show me," I challenge.

I let go, hoping he won't, and wrap my fingers around the base of his thick cock.

Awareness blazes in his eyes, and his hands tighten infinitesimally around my head before gently pushing down.

I smile around his dick as my tongue drags over the metal and down the soft skin until I gag, then repeat the motion.

Hudson immediately loosens his grip until I place one of my hands over his, keeping him there and swallowing.

His responding groan fills the confined space of the limo and clings to my skin as I squirm in front of him. Wanting to give him this. Needing to take it for myself. To know I can. That it's mine to give.

Instinct takes over, and I whimper around him as I drag my lips up and down his shaft.

Every lift of his hips pulls me further under this intoxicating spell of pleasure.

Of desire and need.

Of giving something to this man I want so desperately to take for myself.

When I finally manage to work my lips all the way down to the base of his cock, a string of curses flies from his lips. "I'm gonna come, Madison." He runs his hands through my hair and tugs my head back.

A warning I don't heed as my eyes meet his.

"Fuck . . ." The word is drawn out as salty ropes of hot cum shoot down my throat.

My fist tightens and works in sync with my bobbing head, milking him as he utters words of praise I never knew would have me preening at his feet but have me delirious to do this again.

Once he's spent, he tucks himself back in and pulls me up onto his lap. His mouth covers mine, and his teeth bite into my bottom lip and tug. "I want to take you home now," he growls as a hand wraps around my throat, and his thumb rests on my wildly beating pulse.

I press a finger against his lips. "A lot of people are coming to this bar to celebrate with you tonight, King. You're the man of the hour. You've got to make an appearance."

He sucks my finger into his mouth, and a tingle shoots straight down to my core.

"Fine, but we're not staying long." His thumb presses down gently before his lips touch mine.

"Whatever you say, King."

An hour later, Hudson is standing behind the main bar on the first floor of Kingdom, singing along to "American Pie" with a microphone in one hand and a drink in the other. His smile stretches wide across his face as he feeds off the wild energy in the bar.

"What the fuck, Sawyer? Don't you have some ownery things to do or something?" Chloe glares at Hudson's brother, who hasn't left my side since Hudson was pulled away earlier. "Or have you turned into a stalker?"

"Ownery?" I ask, then turn to Sawyer, who's ignoring Chloe completely.

He laughs at Hudson's kinda awful singing voice, then

flicks his eyes over Chloe. "Listen up, firecracker. . . My brother asked me to make sure his girl was taken care of tonight. It's called loyalty. Not stalking."

"Firecracker," Chloe bristles. "What the hell—" Luckily, Carys interrupts Chloe's tirade and walks over just then, grabbing her to go dance.

"Come on, Mads. Let's dance." I look between the girls, then at the man behind the bar and shake my head no.

"I'm good. You have fun." I raise my bottle to my lips and take a long sip of the cold water, hoping to cool down as I watch the girls get lost on the dance floor. "Why do you antagonize her?" I ask Sawyer. The two of them have been snappy toward each other since we got to the fight earlier.

His grin evokes reminders of a devilish little boy who probably enjoyed torturing his sisters. "Because it's fun."

"Well, I'm a big girl, Sawyer. You don't need to babysit me all night. But thank you for the offer."

He laughs at me.

Legit—laughs in my face.

"It doesn't work that way, Maddie. You came with Hud. He asked me to make sure you were good because he knew he'd be pulled in a million directions tonight. So that's exactly what I'm doing. You're one of us now, and we take care of our own."

I'm sorry. What?

I shake my head, certain I hadn't heard that right. "I'm not one of you, Sawyer. I'm not sure anyone can really be one of you." The Kingstons are intimidating individually. But when you put them all together . . . They rise to an entirely different level.

"Tell yourself whatever you need to, Maddie, but I know my brother." His patronizing smile is easy to read and not so shockingly confident.

My stomach does a weird flip before the song ends, and

Hudson hops over the bar, landing in front of me. His big arm wraps around my bare shoulders, and my skin breaks out in goosebumps at the contact as I'm pulled against him, like it's the most natural thing in the world. "Don't let Sawyer try to steal you away, Mads." Then he stage-whispers, "He's got a micropenis."

"Fuck off, Hud," Sawyer laughs before he brings his eyes back to mine. "Remember what I said, Maddie. See you guys at the game tomorrow."

I ignore Sawyer and look up at the sinfully sexy fighter beside me. "The game?"

"Yeah . . ." he shrugs. "Scarlet asked me to bring you to the family's box at Kings Stadium tomorrow to watch the game with us. I figured since you go every week, anyway, maybe you'd be okay watching with us this time."

The overly confident, animated man who sang to a bar full of people a minute ago is gone and replaced by someone willing to show he's nervous to ask me this. And that, by itself, is incredibly attractive. He's a contradiction. Strong and fierce. Willing to beat someone unconscious in a cage, but he's careful with me.

Soft. Gentle. Patient.

I love it.

That thought flashes across my brain in neon yellow lights, and I nearly choke on it.

I reach up and gently touch the bruise under his eye that's been deepening for the past two hours. "You're lucky I have my Dixon jersey in my bag."

His brows shoot up. "You were planning on leaving me for your brother tomorrow?"

"Nope. I told Brandon I didn't know if I'd make it to the game but I'd watch it on TV. It's a shame you made plans because we could have had a lot of fun during the commercial breaks." I lift up on my toes and softly press my lips to the bruise.

"And then there's half-time." I kiss the small cut on his cheek bone, then the tender spot under his ear before I drag my teeth along the shell and squeal as I'm lifted in the air and thrown over his shoulder.

"We're leaving," he announces to anyone near us as he carries me out of the club. "I'm done waiting, Madison."

Heat builds within me at his declaration.

"Me too, Hudson. Me too."

Hudson

The drive from Kingdom to my house doesn't take long, but Maddie and I spend every second of it making out like two teenagers who just figured out what feels good.

Newsflash—the answer is her. It might have always been her.

When the limo stops at the end of my driveway, and the driver opens our door, my girl smiles and adjusts the laces and silk she calls a shirt, so it covers all the important parts, before carefully sliding out of the back and thanking the driver.

I grab our bags, grateful someone thought to toss them in here earlier, and take her hand in mine.

Maddie shivers in the cold as the limo pulls away and smiles the most beautiful smile I've ever seen. "Look," she holds her hand up as fat snowflakes hit her palm. "It's starting to snow again. Do you think we'll get a decent amount this time?"

I kiss the palm of her hand. "Doubt it." She shivers again and wraps an arm around my waist. "Let's get you inside before you get cold."

"Pretty sure you could keep me warm, King." She bats those damn lashes at me, and I'm sunk.

I hurry us into the house, drop our bags next to the door, then lift her, wrapping her toned legs around my waist. Her mouth is on mine without hesitation. This is the version of Maddie I'm not quite used to but need more of.

My adrenaline high from the night still courses through my veins as I lean her against the door, my hands going everywhere. Her ass. Her waist. Her ribs. I want to trace her tattoo with my tongue. Want to wrap her thighs around my face. Want to learn what makes her scream and shake with need.

Her hands are just as greedy as mine, grabbing and holding. Tracing and squeezing.

I need a goddamn bed to spread her out on, so I can do everything I want to her.

I carry her up the winding stairs and kick open my bedroom door.

Her fingers work to unbutton my shirt when we walk through my room. Soft lips skim along my neck before I drop her down on my bed. Her tits bounce, barely contained in the silk strapless contraption she's wearing, and her words from earlier pique my interest.

What is she wearing under that?

The need builds as I pick up one leg and toss her heel before repeating the action with the other. "You teased me earlier, sunshine."

Maddie's eyes glaze over with a hunger that matches mine, and my cock aches for her against the zipper of my jeans. I regret not having the driver take us home earlier instead of to Kingdom.

Once both her shoes are gone, she shimmies her jeans down her legs, and my breath catches in my throat.

We each have our own colors.

All of Crucible's fighters wear the name, but we do it differently.

Cade's color was green.

Mine have always been royal blue with my name in gold.

It's a play on *king*. It's kitschy, but it's worked.

And tonight, this beautiful woman lying in front of me is wearing my colors. Royal-blue silk is wrapped around her perfect body with thin, shimmering gold threading woven through it. My mouth waters at the possession pounding in my chest and wrapping around my heart.

I run a finger along the lace of her leg. "Jesus Christ, Madison. Are you trying to kill me?"

She sits up and shoves my shirt over my shoulders, then takes my face in her hands and lifts her mouth to mine. The kiss begins softly at first, until I take control and part her lips, licking deep inside her mouth. Then it's possessive and consuming until she's whimpering at the contact and clawing at my skin.

Desperate for more.

Something primal in me snaps. I drink her in, running my fingers through her soft golden locks. Wrapping them around my fist and angling her head for better access.

I need more. *I want everything*.

All of her.

Her body.

Her heart.

Her fucking soul.

I untangle my hand from her hair and shove down my jeans, then drop my knee on the mattress between her legs. With careful, shaking fingers I pull the neckline of the blue silk down under her magnificent tits. Running my tongue lightly around one pale-pink rigid nipple, I hear her breathing falter, then I do it again with more pressure. I suck it into my mouth while my hand cups the other perfect breast. A perfect handful. "How the hell do I get this thing off you, Madison?"

Her back bows off the bed when I tug on her nipple and twist.

"I need more skin," I practically plead while I search for a zipper or a button or a goddamn pair of scissors. *Something*. Anything to get her out of this.

She kisses me slowly with trembling, needy lips, before she flips over onto her knees and tugs on the blue laces that tie in a bow at the small of her back, drawing my eyes down to her delectable ass. Her panties are cut incredibly high on the tight globes of her cheeks. More gold thread shimmers in the lace set off against her creamy skin.

So much creamy skin. "You're killing me," I groan, and she fucking laughs.

It's the sweetest sound, and it grounds me in the moment.

With more patience than I knew I possessed, I take my time unlacing each silk string. Kissing the freckles that dot the soft skin on her shoulders. Exploring each pronounced vertebra of her spine with my tongue. Then with shaking hands, I finally free the last of the lace from her body, rip the corset off her, and suck the skin of the beautiful dimples that sit right above her ass.

A shiver skirts down her skin, and I reach around and palm her breasts before placing another kiss between her shoulder blades and pushing her chest against the bed.

Maddie's delicate fingers fist the blanket.

"Hudson," she keens when I grip her hips between my hands and drag my tongue over the long, lean muscles of her back. My cock grows harder with each inch I taste and every sound she makes.

With careful fingers, I shove the scrap of lace she's calling panties aside and run my nose along her smooth, bare sex. She smells like honey and vanilla, like sex and candy. My mouth waters and goes dry at the same damn time. "So fucking wet for me."

She bucks her hips against my face and moans in response, igniting a fire I never want to extinguish.

I bury my face in her cunt, dragging my tongue up to her clit and fucking feasting like a dying man worshipping at her alter. Licking. Kissing. Tongue-fucking this woman until she's squirming and begging and bucking beneath me.

"Oh God." She smothers her face in the pillows underneath her as the first ripples of her orgasm take control of her and her body starts to shake.

"Let me hear you, Madison." I push a long, thick finger into her wet heat and stretch her.

"Hudson," she pleads, and my name on her lips is an addiction I never want to recover from.

"Give me what I want. Come on my tongue, then I'll let you come on my cock, baby." The demanding words rip from my mouth as I slide a second finger inside her, knuckle-deep, and tongue her harder.

She rocks her hips against my face, and my need to fuck her wars with my need to wring every last shudder I can from her before she takes my cock.

Her body collapses beneath me.

"That's my good girl." I run my hand over the most perfect ass I've ever seen, then flip her over, desperate for more.

"Hudson," she sighs breathlessly. "Please."

I press my lips to hers. "You never have to beg me for anything."

Her hands skim over my body until she can push down my boxers and tilt her hips up to rub against me.

A quake of electricity sends me soaring, and I have to pull away. "I've got to grab a condom, baby."

"You don't, Hud." She rocks against my cock again. "I'm

on the pill, and we both know I'm clean." A pretty blush stains her cheeks. "I trust you."

The weight of her words—of her trust—washes over me, and my chest expands. "Are you sure? I've never gone bare before."

Just the thought of being inside her with nothing between us is enough to set me off.

"Neither have I." A shy smile graces her pretty face and tugs at my heart.

I lean my head against hers and tease her pussy with the head of my cock—running it up and down her drenched sex—while I try to maintain the tiny semblance of control I'm barely grasping right now.

I lean down and kiss her forehead and the corners of her mouth. I dip my tongue between her lips, then graze her chin.

Maddie's nails scrape down my shoulders, over my spine, and then dig into my ass. She wraps her legs around my waist and rocks against me. Silently begging.

Until I finally push the thick head of my dick inside her and hold still. I have to—because nothing has ever felt this good before, and I've barely moved.

She rocks again, and I inch back in warning. "Maddie."

She's so tight. So hot. I have to remind myself that she's never done this before. That I don't want to hurt her. That I have to make this good for her before I take what I want. Before I finally move.

Slowly.

So fucking slowly.

Inch by half inch, I work myself inside her body.

The beating in my chest builds as a heat that's tighter than I've ever experienced before wraps around me like a vice.

She gasps and scores me with her nails.

I press my forehead to hers, ignoring the heavy pressure building at the base of my spine.

Keeping my eyes locked on hers, I push through the tiny bit of resistance and swallow her gasp with a searing kiss.

"Are you okay, sunshine?"

My lips brush over hers again before her soft hands frame my face. "I'm not going to break, Hudson." She licks into my mouth, then whispers, "Fuck me."

MADDIE

Hudson hovers over me, his dark blue eyes sparkling with the strength it's taking for him to stay still while my body adjusts to his. "I'm not going to break, Hudson," I whisper, my breath fanning over the tight line of his chiseled jaw. "Fuck me . . . Please."

"When those filthy words leave that pretty mouth, baby . . ." His voice vibrates deep in his chest as a smile pulls at his sexy lips, and I melt.

I scrape my nails over his taut abs—all eight of them—then dig them into his back until he shifts his hips and presses in until he can't go further.

The pressure inside me builds and pinches until I can't find my breath or my thoughts. Until all I can do is feel. Feel him inside me. Stretching me. Filling me. Holding me.

"Breathe, baby."

But I can't breathe.

I can't move.

I can't speak.

I'm about to be split in two, and it's the sweetest pain I've ever experienced.

The metal balls rub against my inner walls, igniting every nerve ending in their path.

He keeps his head pressed to mine as he devours me. Worships me. Tells me how good I'm doing. How perfect my cunt is. Gradually, every inch of discomfort eases and is replaced with pleasure.

Leaving me breathless and gasping with each snap of his hips and every hungry stroke of his tongue against mine. Electricity arcing and soaring and sparking between us. Our connection is so intense, it consumes me from the tips of my toes to the top of my head.

Pulsing against my skin.

Thrumming through my veins.

Overwhelming my senses as I wrap myself around him.

Pleasure and pain, trust and desire all join together until I can't tell where one stops and the other starts.

Like a storm wrapping around us.

"That's it, baby. Hold on to me." His strong arms slide down and cup my bottom in his hands, digging into the soft skin. He pushes in torturously slow before pulling out in equally lazy movements that are intended to drive me crazy.

Each drag of his cock is more delicious than the last.

Branding me.

Breaking me.

Owning me.

Saving me.

"You're taking my cock like such a good girl, Maddie." He swallows my moan, and a shiver courses through me at his words. "Such a fucking good girl."

A whimper lodges in my throat at the exquisite pain and mind-numbing pleasure.

At the dirty words and my all-consuming reaction to his praise.

I wrap my arms around his shoulders, loving the feeling

of his strong muscles under my hands and the brush of his lips over mine. Our chests press together, and his weight is deliciously heavy against me.

A sound I don't recognize tears from my throat. Raw and visceral as I shatter around him, my toes curling and my thighs shaking. "Hudson," I shriek and inhale as he flips us over so we're both sitting up with me in his lap. My legs wrap around his waist, and my hands fist in his hair.

"That's good, baby. But I want more."

Not so much as a breath of space exists between our bodies.

We're a tangle of limbs, wrapped around each other as he moves me up and down with his strong hands. His hot mouth sucks my breast as he thrusts up, hitting an entirely new spot. My toes curl as he drives himself into me over and over until I don't think I can take anymore.

Our rapid breathing mixes together as pleasure flows thick in my blood.

I willingly relinquish every ounce of control to this man.

Trusting him with my body and my heart.

Drowning in him.

Clinging to him.

Another orgasm builds quickly, threatening to pull me under. To suck all the oxygen from my lungs. "Oh God, Hudson. I can't."

"Yes, you can." He fucks into me over and over with one hand wrapped around my hip, moving me like a rag doll, while the other snakes between us, and a callused finger presses my clit. "Give me another, Madison."

His rough finger rubs in fast circles as he thrusts again, and my walls tighten and clamp down. "Come now, Madison," he demands in a voice that's raspy and sexy and so demanding.

Stars burst behind my eyes, and I come on a silent cry as

wave after wave of mind-blistering pleasure courses through me.

Spent, I cling to him in his arms as his cock pulses inside me.

Never wanting to move. Not sure I could if I tried.

Seconds turn to minutes, and I lose track of time. Lose track of everything but Hudson and me and our beating hearts.

When I finally lift my head from the crook of his neck, tears threaten to spill from my eyes as my emotions overwhelm me.

Hudson doesn't say anything. He just takes my lips in a bruising kiss, then lays me down in his arms, covering my skin with his. "Maddie . . ." he starts, then stops with a soft, reverence to his voice. He kisses me again, and I lift my hands to his face, holding them there.

Unspoken words pass between us, and I press my finger to his lips.

"Me too, Hud," I answer and close my eyes.

"Do you want to go to sleep?" he asks as his fingers trail up and down my side, like he can't get enough. Like he needs to touch me. Like I need him in order to breathe.

I think about that for a minute, then roll over to face him and shake my head. Not ready for the night to end. "I've always wanted to enjoy a hot tub in the snow."

A wicked grin spreads across his face, and I clench my legs together.

A half an hour later, we're bathed in the silvery moonlight as the snow falls around us, while our bodies are submerged in the warmth.

But as I straddle his lap and squeeze his big dick in my hand, Hudson nips at my lips. "You're going to be sore tomorrow, baby."

"Says the big bad fighter," I tease as I lower myself onto him, welcoming the pain.

Pain reminds you you're alive.

His rough palms squeeze my breasts as I begin to move. "Jesus Christ, Madison. Your pussy is fucking perfect." He rolls my nipple between his thumb and finger, and I feel the pull in the very depths of my core.

I hold his shoulders for balance as I rock slowly in his lap, finding the rhythm I want and figuring out what works for me. The frigid air touches more of my skin with each lazy movement.

"Tell me how it feels, Maddie," he demands as one hand slides down my body, gripping my bottom.

"I like that," I murmur.

He licks along my lip before dragging it between his teeth. "Like what, sunshine? Use your words." He thrusts up and smiles.

"Do you like my cock?" Another thrust. "Do you like the way it feels inside your cunt?"

My face heats.

"Do you like the way I stretch this pretty pussy?" This thrust is harder as I throw my head back. "Or the way I grab your ass? Because you have the most perfect fucking ass ever, baby."

"Hud . . ." I whimper.

"I'm gonna take your ass one day, Madison. I'm going to own every inch of your beautiful body, and you're going to fucking beg for it. Beg me to fill you everywhere."

"Oh my God." My breath catches in my throat. "Yes. I want that. Mmm . . . I want all of that. I want you to fill me. I want you to fuck me."

"I want my cum dripping out of you for days. I want you so sore that every step you take makes you think of tonight and the way my cock feels inside your perfect fucking cunt."

"Oh, God . . ." His words push me over the edge, and I cry out, "Yes. Fuck. Fuck. Fuck."

Hudson stands and drops me to my feet, then turns me around and bends me over the edge of the hot tub and slams into me from behind, his lips on my spine and his hips pistoning into me. His piercing threatens to shred me to pieces, but I don't think I could have stopped him if I wanted to. And I *never* want him to stop.

"Maddie . . . Fuck, Maddie." He buries his face in my neck, sucking the soft spot there, and the now-familiar flutters that had only just died down detonate behind my eyes.

I can't see. Can't breathe as my climax tears through me, ripping from my lungs and coursing through my veins.

Hudson's entire body tightens, then fills me as he comes with my name on his lips.

His voice envelops me like a warm blanket I want to wrap myself up in.

If this is a dream, I never want to wake.

We tumble into bed sated and exhausted.

My muscles are sore, and my heart pounds inside my chest.

This is crazy . . . right?

Hudson brushes over my dragonfly tattoo, tracing the lines and watercolor splashes first with his thumb, then his finger, and finally, with a delicate, worshipping kiss. "You gonna tell me about this?"

I curl into him as he fingers it lovingly. "Why a dragonfly, sunshine?"

"Why do you call me sunshine?" I counter.

"Because you are, baby. You're sunshine and warmth. Your smile, your eyes, your entire fucking being lights up every room you walk into, and you don't even realize it. I've always wanted to be near you. Been drawn to you. Always wanted just a piece of your attention, so I could feel your warmth."

My breath is caught in my throat at his admission. "Hudson . . ." I run my nails over the sleeve tattooed on his arm. "The dragonfly is a symbol. I read about them my freshman year of high school, and it always stuck with me. They're a symbol of change and transformation. Adaptability. All the things that were so important to surviving while I was growing up. But they're also delicate and beautiful. Their strength is hidden. I guess I just always felt connected to that. As soon as I saved the money, a friend and I snuck out and got tattoos. I liked that I could hide it and that it was just for me."

"I fucking love it, Maddie." His lips press against my skin. "You are the strongest woman I've ever met. I hope you know that, sunshine." He yawns and curls his arms tighter around me. "I love your strength and your warmth, and your sass." We lie tangled in each other as I run my fingers through his hair, only stopping when he eventually falls asleep. His blond hair falls into his eyes but fails to hide the bruising that bloomed purple, high on his cheek. I was thankful the fight had only gone one round this time, since I didn't know how I'd handle my nerves wracking me longer than that.

How are you supposed to watch someone you . . . *care about* . . . get hurt?

I lay awake all night, thinking about his life and what it would mean to be part of it.

How does his family do it?

How do they watch this man in fight after fight?

Year after year?

And *oh God*, his family.

Am I really being thrown to the wolves tomorrow? Because in a lot of ways, that's exactly what the Kingstons are. Apex predators who run in a very elite pack. How are they going to handle him bringing someone who's so far out of his league, let alone his tax bracket, into their inner sanctum?

They have an owner's box at Kings Stadium, but that's not where the family watches the games. The Kingstons like their privacy and keep a separate suite just for the family.

My stomach lurches at the thought, and I wrap my arm around Hudson's waist, tucking my face against his chest.

I used to hold my own against new foster families, new schools, new mean girls, and new handsy boys all the time. I can handle the Kingstons. At least, that's what I try to convince myself before I finally fall asleep.

I press my lips gently to the scrolling font inked on his chest.

Only the good die young.

I used to think that was true, but now I'm praying I'm wrong.

This man is worth living for.

When I step into the kitchen the next morning, dressed for the game, Hudson whistles like I'm wearing lingerie and high heels and not my black-and-gold Philadelphia Kings jersey with my matching black Converse sneakers sporting sparkly gold laces. He motions for me to spin around, and I laugh at him and walk into his open arms instead.

"You look damn good, sunshine. We could always skip the game." His fingers thread through my hair as he kisses me.

I sigh, contentment in the moment flowing through me, and he deepens the kiss with a hot stroke of his tongue.

Within seconds, I'm clinging to him, addicted to this feeling —this all-consuming need for Hudson Kingston. "I'm fine with staying here to watch it, but one way or another, I'm watching my brother play, King."

"Fine," he pouts. "Where's your coat?"

I shrug. "I didn't bring one."

"Swear to God, Madison. There's two inches of snow on the ground, and you don't have a coat? What am I going to do with you?" He wraps his peacoat around my shoulders and kisses me again.

"I can think of a few things. But they'll have to wait until after the game." I brush my lips over the scruff on his chin and hum. "We'll have a few hours before I need to get back to my house tonight."

His face falls. "You're not sleeping here tonight?"

"I thought I was going home." My eyes search his face for guidance. "Hud, you've got to remember I've never done this before. This whole . . . I don't know, relationship thing. I don't know what I'm supposed to do."

"That makes two of us, Mads. We'll figure it out together. We'll do what feels right for us." He runs his hands over the back of my head, and I nearly swoon, unsure if he could possibly say anything more perfect than that.

HUDSON

Maddie Facetimed with Daphne as we drove to the game. It was funny listening to this side of the conversation. Daphne was giving her the lowdown on how to handle my family like an old pro, and my chest expanded, yet again, for my brother's wife. For the way she was boosting Maddie's confidence. And for the hesitance I recognized in her voice when she started talking about being initiated into our family.

I like that my girl found her tribe, and that they're fiercely protective of each other.

We valet park at Kings Stadium, and I hold her hand in mine as we walk in, greeting most of the security and vendors as we go.

It's been a few years since Scarlet took over control of the Kings from Max when he moved over to the Revolution hockey team. One of the first things she did was buy the new family suite to insulate us from the constant eyes of reporters and guests, who were always present when we watched the game from my father's owner's box back in the day.

It was how we'd all grown up.

Constantly having to be *on*.

To behave a certain way.

To carefully curate the way we spoke, what we wore, and the things we said.

To be part of the Kingston brand, not just part of the family.

She didn't want to raise her kids in that environment. She didn't want any of us to have to do that. And suddenly, we didn't. During football season, Sunday family dinners are at the stadium in this box. Admittedly, it's a little different from your typical family when you consider where we are and what we're doing. But it's also that we all try to make it to as many home games as we can, just to be with each other, that makes it special. Playpens and toys are scattered around the room for the kids. Brynlee insisted on a swear jar that sits on the bar each week, and when Maddie and I walk in, I retrieve a twenty-dollar bill from my wallet and drop it in.

"What are you doing?" she asks before anyone realizes we're even here.

"Prepaying the swear jar." And with that announcement, the horde swarms.

Max and Daphne are the only ones not here today, which leaves a whole lot of my family to contend with. Within seconds, Lenny has an arm linked through Maddie's as she tugs her toward Amelia and Scarlet, who are sitting in the corner with babies crawling around their legs. If Maddie doesn't want to be touched by my family, she better speak up now because we're a touchy-feely bunch. But she doesn't say a word. Just spares me a quick, forced smile and lets my sister drag her away.

Becket waves a beer in front of my face to get my attention. "Come on, champ. She's only across the room."

"Fuck off, Becks." I take the beer from his hand, and we

join Jace, Sawyer, Cade and our brother-in-law, Sam, who happens to be both Amelia's husband and Lenny's husband's older brother.

We stand in front of the window of the box and watch the team line up on the field. Len's husband, Sebastian, takes his spot out there, and Lenny points with Maverick's hand toward the glass. "Wave to Daddy." Mav claps, and my smile grows.

Guess the little dude is finally sleeping again.

"How are you feeling?" Jace asks, and I sip my beer while wicked thoughts of last night come to mind.

I clear my throat and stifle a laugh. "I'm good."

Cade glares as he takes a long pull from his bottle of beer.

"Knock it off, Saint. The fight is over. And the *no women* rule will never work again."

Becks looks between me and Cade. "And why is that?"

It's my turn to take a long pull of my beer, then look over at Maddie. She's laughing at something Lenny has said and already has Amelia and Sam's daughter, Caitlin, sitting in her lap. *She's my why.* "Because she's mine," I tell the group.

Everyone starts talking all at once. Wallets are pulled out, and money is exchanged. Sawyer ends up with all of it in his hand as he thanks me.

"What the actual fuck?" I ask, having no clue what the hell just happened. But Cade's scowl has just turned into a shit-eating grin.

"I thought you'd at least wait a week, shithead. You just lost me enough money to feed the fucking swear jar for six months," Cade groans and shoves his wallet back in his pocket, then bends down to pick up Killian, who's just wandered over with a toy football in his hands.

"Not me, brother." Sawyer counts his money. "I knew you were done for."

Jace shoves two crisp hundred-dollar bills in Sawyer's

palm. "I fucking knew it too, but I thought it would take him longer than this to figure it out. Fucking Philadelphia's most eligible bachelor, and you just blew your load in one damn shot."

I smack the back of his head. "Watch it, jackoff," then mutter under my breath, "*It was way more than once.*"

Sam hands over his money, shaking his head. Sam never loses. "When did you think I'd get my head out of my ass?" I ask, knowing Sam knows fucking everything.

"I didn't think you'd make it to the fight. I thought you'd figure it out last week." He taps his crystal bourbon glass to my beer. "Amelia likes her."

"I didn't realize Amelia knew Maddie that well." I look over at her again, and I swear to God, it's like my chest hurts just looking at her.

Sam shrugs. "Maddie handles Sweet Temptations' social-media accounts."

After a few plays, Maddie stands and cheers when her brother tackles a guy so hard, he has to be carried off the field.

"Try not to piss this one off, Hud." Scarlet moves in next to me. "I think she's got a hidden mean streak." She watches Maddie, who seems to be explaining football to my niece, who's too young to walk or talk in complete sentences yet.

"There's not a mean bone in her body, Scar. But she's loyal to a fault and would go to war for her brother." I throw my arm around my older sister. "Kinda like another woman I know."

Scarlet levels me with an intimidating scowl. "Don't fuck up my reputation, Hudson. I'm scary. It stops there. Period. Keep the mushy stuff to yourself."

"Whatever you say, sis." I turn back to the bar. "Want another drink?" I ask, eyeing the water bottle in her hand suspiciously. "No wine today, Scar? You feeling okay?"

Jace walks over to us and smirks. "She turned down the sushi earlier too."

Becks spins around. "Again? Can't we have a single year without crazy and emotional pregnant sisters?"

Scarlet pours the remnants of her water bottle over his head. "Nope."

Becket's eyes practically pop out of his head as he wipes the water from his face. "I was fucking kidding."

"Are you really pregnant?" Sawyer stands between Scarlet and Becks, trying to limit the carnage. When her eyes water as she shakes her head, Cade wraps her in his arms and whispers in her ear while we all stand there, dumbstruck.

My sister is an ice queen.

Always has been.

But damn, she's an emotional pregnant person.

Maddie crosses the room and slides in next to me to congratulate them. And I love that she's here for this. I stare at her for a minute. At the way the sunlight is hitting her golden hair. At her beautiful smile. At those damn freckles I want to kiss, and the dimples in her cheeks that tell me she's genuinely happy right now. Then it dawns on me. I don't love that she's here for this. I love *her*.

The thought hits me like a sucker punch to the jaw.

Holy shit.

She really is it for me.

It's like my world tilts on its axis for a moment before righting itself again.

She's it. She's the center. She's the sun.

My phone vibrates in my pocket, but I ignore it and wrap my arm around her, rubbing my thumb over the spot covering her tattoo. And an idea forms. Until my fucking phone vibrates again.

Maddie looks up at me when I pull it from my pocket,

and I can't help myself. I brush a quick kiss over her lips and step away to answer my agent.

"Hunter, man. What's going on?" I ask, but a long moment passes without him saying anything. "Hunter?"

"Hudson, I got some bad news this morning." Shit. My stomach drops. The last time he said that to me, someone had gotten pictures of me and a one-night stand from Vegas—probably from her fucking phone—that we had to buy back so they couldn't be sold to any of those shitty celebrity magazines.

"Whatever it is, Hunt, just deal with it if you can. I'm enjoying my win. I'm enjoying my family. I'm not ready to think about work."

"Are you at the game, Hud?" he asks, and I realize what I hear in the background. Hunter was in town last night for the fight, but he represents a few of the guys on the Kings team. He's probably in the owner's box right now.

"Yeah, man. I'm here." I look around the room at all the smiling faces—except Maddie's, who's watching me and has already tuned in to something being wrong.

There's a knock at the door before security moves aside to let Hunter in.

Heads swing our way as my family realizes someone has just joined us. Hunter lifts his chin toward my family, and Cade and Scarlet immediately walk over to him, followed by Lenny. Her husband is one of Hunter's clients.

"Hey, guys. Could you give Hudson and me a moment?" Hunter asks but then changes his mind. "Actually . . ." He turns back to me. "Up to you, man. Do you want them to stay?"

"What the fuck, Hunt? What's going on?" I feel Maddie before she makes it to my side and links her fingers through mine.

"I just got a call from Mason McGuire's agent." Hunter's tone drops low, and my stomach drops with it.

"Does he want a rematch already?" Jace asks.

"No," Hunter answers carefully. "He's dead."

I take a step back. Floored. "What happened? He was fine after the fight last night."

This can't be right.

The noise in the suite comes to a standstill. Someone must have asked them to shut off the audio pumping in from the stadium. The only thing I hear is my heart racing.

"According to his agent, he wasn't feeling right last night, and his wife made him go to the hospital sometime around midnight. But it was too late. They did a CT angiogram when he wasn't improving after a few hours, but the damage had been done, and he bled out before they could get him into surgery."

I fall into the seat behind me and drop Maddie's hand.

"It wasn't your fault, King. They called it a berry aneurysm. It was a defect in the lining of his blood vessels in his brain. He was a walking time bomb. It's amazing he managed to fight this long." Hunter might say something else, but the buzzing in my head drowns him out.

All I hear was that I killed Mason McGuire.

Maddie

Hudson's family goes into crisis mode while he sits quietly, in shock.

If I had to guess, he's completely numb.

They're all talking over each other as Scarlet and Becket both try to take control.

I look between all of them and decide to go for Sawyer. "We need to get him out of here."

Sawyer turns to me, quiet for a second before realization dawns. "You're right. Can we take him to your house? Once the news gets hold of this, they'll have his place and Crucible surrounded."

Scarlet overhears our conversation and joins us. "You're right, Maddie. He needs to leave now. Why don't you two take him back to your house, and Jace . . ." She grabs the back of his hoodie and drags him toward us. "You need to go get a bag from Hudson's place and take it to Maddie's." She shoves him away. "Go now. Maddie will text you the address."

He looks between his sister and me, then nods and walks out the door.

"Hand me your phone." Scarlet holds her hand out, waiting, and I do as I'm told. Her fingers run over the screen before she hands it back to me. "Jace's contact is in there. Text him your address."

I stare at my phone before lifting my eyes to hers with a newfound respect. She's not as scary as I used to think, now that I see her in this light. She's in protection mode, the way Brandon always is, and I get it in a different way than I ever have before.

I wrap my fingers around my phone, but she holds tight. "Can you handle this, Madison?"

I grab the phone from her fingers and meet her eyes. "Watch me," I tell her before looking at Hudson, who's sitting there, looking broken.

A slow smile spreads across her face. "Nothing like baptism by fire. Welcome to the family." She turns away from me and kisses her husband, then turns to Hud's agent. "Hunter, let's go downstairs to my office. We're going to need a game plan."

Sawyer hugs his sister. "Call me when you've got a plan."

He moves to where Hudson's sitting, but Hud doesn't

look up until I join them and take his hands in mine. "Come on, King. Let's go home."

This man doesn't say a word to me or anyone else. He just stands and lets me take his hand as we follow Sawyer out of the stadium and into his sleek sports car.

I text my brother and let him know what's happening and to expect some Kingstons to be at the house when he gets home, hoping not to catch him too off guard. Then I tuck myself in next to Hudson for the drive. He still hasn't said anything, but he wraps his arm around me and holds onto me like a lifeline.

That changes when we get to the house.

The three of us walk in, but Hudson heads right out into the backyard. When I move to follow him, Sawyer grabs my shoulder, and I manage not to knee him in the nuts. "Give him some space, Maddie."

I peel his finger from my shoulder and look him straight in the eyes. "Don't ever assume a woman is okay with being touched, Sawyer. You don't know me. So I'll give you that this time. But don't tell me what to do either."

"Damn," he whistles. "I thought you were the quiet one."

"Being quiet and choosing not to say anything are two completely different things. I like you. You seem like a good guy, and anyone with eyes can see how tightly knit your family is, but you're not stopping me from going out there." I take a step toward the sliding-glass doors before Sawyer calls out my name.

"Maddie . . . Don't let him freeze you out. Hudson's good at shutting down."

It won't be the first time I've had to fight for something I've wanted in my life.

When I step outside, Hudson has the phone to his ear, and he's yelling at Hunter.

"I want her goddamned number, Hunt. He has a pregnant

wife. I want to talk to her." He looks over at me, then gives me his back as he listens to whatever Hunter says. "I don't care. Get me her number and get me her address. They're local." He ends the call and shoves his phone in his pocket.

"Hudson . . ." I approach slowly, like I would a wounded animal. "Can I get you anything?"

He shakes his head no but won't look at me.

I slip his peacoat off my shoulders and hand it to him. "If you're going to stay out here in the snow, will you put this on for me?" I tack on a *please*, then stand there and wait until he slips his arms through it and walks away.

Sawyer and I are sitting at the kitchen counter, having tea, when someone knocks on the door. Then Jace lets himself inside my home.

My jaw hits the floor. "You know, when you knock, it's customary to wait until someone opens the door before you just walk into a house, right?"

The giant hockey player grins. "Family doesn't knock." He holds up Hudson's bag. "Where should I put this?"

"My door's open at the top of the stairs," I tell him before Sawyer walks into the room, and Cinder decides to wind herself through his legs before moving on to Jace and swishing her tail at him while she purrs.

Yeah, girl, I know. These men are blessed with some incredible genes.

"Don't trust him in your room, Maddie. He might steal your underwear." Sawyer takes the bag from Jace and punches him in the arm before he walks up the stairs.

Jace turns to me. "It was one fucking time, and in all fairness, she's a fucking supermodel now."

"Oh, gross." I take a step back from him and stare. "I don't want to know."

He shrugs and looks around, his face turning serious. "Where's Hudson?"

"He's outside. He wanted space." My heart cracks a little at the admission, and Jace slings his arm around my shoulder. "Seriously . . . what's with you guys and touching?"

"What?" he asks, looking at me like I've lost my mind. "I'm not hitting on you."

I roll my eyes and silently beg for strength when the back door opens and Hudson walks in. He shakes off his coat and lays it over a chair, then kicks off his wet sneakers. "Hunter is going to come over. Is that okay, Mads?"

I nod my head but don't move.

Hudson's eyes focus on Jace's arm around my shoulder. He crosses the room and smacks him off. "She doesn't like to be touched, asshole."

"She's part of the family now," Jace counters, and my mind spins.

Since when?

"Keep your fucking hands to yourself," Hudson growls as Sawyer walks back into the room. "Have either of you talked to Scarlet?"

"Yeah, brother." Sawyer pulls his phone out and opens his texts. "She'll be here soon and says don't talk to anyone until she gets here."

There's a knock at the front door, and Jace answers it, like he belongs here. Then he lets Hudson's agent, Hunter, and a beautiful woman into my house. *Jesus.* How many of them are there?

"Maybe I should order some food." I don't wait for an answer before walking into the kitchen and grabbing the menu from the local sandwich shop.

HUDSON

*H*unter introduces his wife, Skylar, to my brothers as Maddie walks away, and the walls start closing in on me.

I've met Skye a few times. She's a neurosurgeon in New York City, so I decide maybe she's the answer I'm looking for. "Skye, can you explain to me how this happens? How does someone go from healthy and awake last night to dead this morning. What the hell happened?"

What I really want to ask is *what did I do?*

"Is there somewhere we can sit?" she asks. We all move to the dining-room table, and she pulls an old envelope and a pen from her purse, then draws something and starts pointing to it and explaining. "Berry aneurysms aren't that uncommon. They're a defect in the lining of one of the blood vessels of the brain. At this spot, the vessel wall has weakened and thinned, causing it to bulge out like a balloon. Most people walk around with absolutely no idea they have this sitting in their brain, like a ticking time bomb waiting to go off." She stops speaking, but I already know Maddie's walked back into the room. I can feel her eyes on me. But I don't look at her. I can't.

Skylar stands from the table and reaches out to Maddie. "Hi. I'm Skylar Carter. Hunter's wife."

"Nice to meet you, Skylar. I'm Maddie . . ." She leaves the rest unsaid, and I cringe.

Yeah. I wouldn't want to admit I was with a murderer either.

Hunter smiles at Maddie. "Nice to see you again, Maddie. Brandon played a great game today."

I guess he's Dixon's agent too.

"Thanks, Hunter. Can I get you guys anything?" When Hunt shakes his head no, she pulls out the chair next to me. "Please don't stop. What were you saying?" Maddie asks Skye.

But Hunter is the one that answers, and he's only looking at me. "She's trying to tell you this wasn't your fault, Hudson. You couldn't have known."

"Tell that to his pregnant wife." I stand, not sure where I'm going when the front door opens, and Dixon steps aside, letting Scarlet in, who's followed by Cade.

I ignore my sister and coach.

Not in the mood for more of the *it's not your fault* line and make my way to Dixon instead. "Hey, man. Do you have a gym here?"

He drops his bag at his feet, still dressed in his game-day suit. "Yeah. Come on."

No questions asked, he opens a different door, and I follow him down a set of stairs to a state-of-the-art gym. My eyes trail over the heavy bag hanging in one corner and the free weights stacked neatly near a bench in the other.

"You want some help down here, King?" Dixon removes his jacket, ready to roll up his sleeves and help however I need, but I shake my head no.

"Can you just make sure Maddie's okay?" I ask, not at all in the mood for company.

"You coming upstairs any time soon?" Cade asks as he walks down the basement steps.

I drop the hex bar at my feet, having lost count of my reps an hour ago. "Wasn't planning on it." I wipe the sweat away from my eyes and stare back at my coach.

"Hudson . . . this wasn't—"

"Save it, Cade. I don't want to hear it. Not now. Can you just get everyone out of here? Can I deal with the crisis PR mode tomorrow? Because tonight, I can't fucking deal with the war room I have no doubt my sister set up upstairs."

I grab the bar in both hands, ignoring the sting of the open-blistered calluses on the pads of my palm.

"Hudson."

"Tomorrow, Saint. Help me get through the fucking night with this blood on my hands and get everyone out of this fucking house. Do it for me, like you know I'd do it for you," I plead.

Fucking exhausted.

But not tired enough to forget.

"Imogen's been calling all night." His voice is softer when he mentions his sister.

One more person I let down.

"Tomorrow. Please, coach." I pick the hex bar back up and start another rep of deadlifts instead of waiting for him to answer.

Cade stands there watching me for a while, his arms crossed over his chest and leaning against a pillar by the stairs, before eventually accepting that I don't want to talk and finally leaving me alone.

I'm not sure how many hours go by or how many reps I do before I give up.

The anger doesn't pass. It's there under everything.

The pain hasn't stopped. It's just dulled.

But I still see that hit over and over in my mind.

The way my knee made contact with his face.

A quiet gasp catches me off guard as I turn around and wipe my hands on my pants. Maddie is sitting on the bottom step, her arms wrapped around her knees and silent, fat tears clinging to her dark lashes. She rushes toward me and grabs a towel from a shelf, then wraps it around my bloody palms. "You've gotta stop, Hudson. I refuse to sit here and let you hurt yourself."

This woman is so good and pure that, for a moment, I let her clean my hands, then tuck herself against my chest. Soaking her in before I push her away.

"Hudson?" Confusion glistens in her bright blue eyes as they flash with hurt.

I answer her quietly, not wanting to hear my own voice. "I need to go home, Mads. I can't stay here."

Even if I want to.

Even if I wish I could.

The questions torturing me since I heard the news of McGuire's death play on a constant loop in my mind. How am I supposed to live with the fact that I killed a man? Could I have done something different? How can I ever touch her with hands that ended someone's life?

Maddie presses her lips to my sweat-drenched chest before lifting on her toes and wrapping her arms around my shoulders. "If you want to go home, I'm going with you."

"There's probably press everywhere, Maddie." My gut tightens at the thought of them invading my space and getting near her.

Her thumb runs gently over the small cut on my cheek.

"Then I guess you better stay here . . . with me." She lowers back down and takes both my hands in hers, placing a kiss to each open palm. "I have no idea what you're going through, Hudson. I can't even begin to fathom it. But I'm not going to let you go through it alone."

She tugs on my wrist, trying to get me to move with her. "Everyone is gone."

So fucking pure.

When I don't move, a silent fury burns in her eyes. "Don't you dare, Hudson Kingston. I'm not some delicate flower that's going to wilt when things get tough. Now, come with me."

I grab my shirt from the floor and follow her up the stairs, having no energy left to fight.

I have no idea what tomorrow will bring, but I'm not ready to figure it out now.

Maddie

I tug Hudson up the stairs behind me, careful not to touch his hands. Then I push him into my en suite bathroom and turn on the shower. But before I get him in there, I force him down on the closed toilet and grab my first aid kit from under the sink.

"I'm fine, Mads," Hudson mumbles as I take his hands.

That might be what this man wants to believe, but the hiss that escapes when I pour the alcohol over the raw pads of his palms tells me something completely different. Once they're cleaned, I pull him to his feet and shove his jeans down, then do the same with his boxers and socks before I push him into the shower and follow behind him a minute later.

Hudson doesn't say anything.

Not a single word.

But he doesn't push me away.

I run my loofah over his arms and chest. Down his abs and over his back. It's not supposed to be sexual, but it's impossible to miss how his cock grows hard and heavy between his legs when I gently rub his piercings.

"Maddie." My name is a quiet, strangled cry from his lips. "I don't feel anything. I'm numb. I killed a man. What kind of monster am I?"

I curl my arms around his shoulders and kiss him with every ounce of pain and fear I've been holding on to today. Knowing what he needs. "Feel me, Hudson. I'm here. I'm with you, and you are not a monster."

I deepen the kiss with a desperation. It's furious. It's rough and messy. Our tongues collide as the world around us disappears, leaving just the two of us.

Hudson boosts me up and leans me against the cool tile wall. Hot water sprays down on us as I wrap my legs around his waist and lower myself onto his thick cock.

He tries going slow, no doubt worried about hurting me, but I dig my heels into his backside, knowing soft and slow isn't what he needs now. Then I roll my hips over the hard length of him.

A guttural groan rips from his chest, and he holds himself still. "I can't, Maddie. I don't want to hurt you."

The hot water pounds down on my face when we kiss again. "You can, Hudson. Take what you need. Please. Let me help you. Let me in," I beg.

This man holds me like I weigh nothing in his arms.

As if he hadn't spent the last three hours in the gym after the worst day of his life.

His hold tightens around me as he shifts in slowly, then pulls out again.

"Fuck me, Hudson," I whisper into his ear.

"You don't know what you're asking." His dark pupils are blown wide with need. He's on the verge of snapping, and I whimper.

"I need you too, Hud. Show me you're here with me. That you're all right. Please."

Quickly, Hud lifts me higher against the wall of the shower, then pistons his hips, pounding almost violently into me.

Every muscle in his body straining and pulling.

Flexing and shaking.

His face tight and his eyes unfocused.

Quickly, the now-familiar sensation of my impending orgasm catches fire and shatters. Hudson follows me over the edge, and my name is whispered like a silent plea for mercy.

For forgiveness.

This isn't the version of Hudson Kingston he shows the world.

But I love it all. All the versions. All of this man.

MADDIE

"We've really got to stop meeting like this." I knew from the knock at the front door that Sawyer was here. He seems to be the early morning Kingston.

He squeezes my hand as he walks by, heading for the kitchen. "What's for breakfast today, Mads?"

Two weeks ago, I would have lost my mind if anyone took it upon themselves to touch me as much as the Kingston siblings do. But I guess in a way, it's immersion therapy.

Kind of like a baby being thrown into the deep end of the pool, not that I'm saying you should do that. But in those videos, they either swim or need to be saved. And I'm tired of needing to be saved. So even though my first instinct may be to back away, I don't. Not with any of them. And they've *all* been in my house over the past few days.

It's basically been a parade of well-meaning siblings.

"Is he awake yet?" Sawyer helps himself to a mug and pours a cup of coffee.

I swear, I may never get used to this. For the longest time, my happy bubble consisted of Brandon, the girls, and Watkins . . . and that worked. Now that bubble has popped, and the Kingstons have invaded.

They're kinda like gremlins.

They're a little mischievous.

They seem to speak their own language.

They multiply when you're not looking, almost always traveling in packs.

Yesterday, Jace stopped by after his hockey practice at Kroydon University, told me he was starving, and then answered my door ten minutes later. He returned to the kitchen with takeout he'd DoorDashed for all of us. "I wasn't sure if you ate pasta or not, Mads. Hud said the pasta messes with your sugar." He proudly held up the bags with a goofy grin. "So I got a few different options and also a chicken Caesar salad." He laid out enough food for an army, then yelled up the stairs for Hudson and Brandon to come eat, like he lived here.

"Maddie . . ." Sawyer waves his hand in front of my face, bringing me back to the current Kingston invading my space, and I blink away the fog.

I . . . I'm so tired.

"Sorry, Sawyer." I shake my head and look at the closed door to the basement. "Hudson's up. He's in the gym."

"Does he know the funeral is today?"

I recall the fight he had with Hunter yesterday. "Yeah. He knows. He wants to go. Hunter told him it's a bad idea. But Hud said he'd stay at the very back of the crowd. He feels like he needs to be there—that he owes Mason that."

"Damn." Sawyer leans back against the counter and stares at the floor. "Are you going with him?"

I nod.

"I'm worried about him, Maddie."

I wish I could tell Sawyer he doesn't need to worry. But I

can't. Everyone's been here. All the Kingstons. Cade. Cooper. Imogen. For days now, our house has been a revolving door of people who care about Hudson. But for some reason, my brother is the only person I've seen him open up to.

"Trauma is a tricky thing. He'll talk about it when he's ready. Until then, we need to be patient." The way he's always been patient with me.

"Scarlet said he's probably safe to go home now." Sawyer eyes me over the rim of his coffee cup.

"Cooper told us last night. He said most of the reporters have cleared off the street." My heart pangs at the idea of Hudson going home because I'm not sure if he'll push me away when he finally can.

The signs are there. I may be inexperienced, but I'm not blind.

He's closed himself off.

Not just from his siblings and friends but from me too.

"Are you sure you want to do this?" I ask as I flatten my hands over his silver tie.

Hudson is sitting on my bed while I stand between his legs. The black suit that was dropped off earlier fits him beautifully. "No one would think any less of you if we skip this today."

His hands rest gently on my hips when he drops his head to my chest and inhales deeply. "I have to do this, Mads."

I run my nails over the back of his head and hold him to me. Fighting against every inch he slips away. "Okay. Then we need to leave now. The church is an hour north of here."

I pull him to his feet and turn away, but his grip slips to my hands, and he tugs me back. "I think I should go home after the funeral."

Here it comes.

"Alone," he adds, and even though I knew it was coming, it still hurts.

I step further into his space and lift my chin. "No."

"What?" He drops my hands, so I lift them to the lapel of his suit coat and curl my fingers into the expensive material.

"I said no." My voice shakes, betraying my fraying nerves. "You're not going home alone. I'm not leaving you alone. If you're not ready to talk, that's fine. Then don't talk. If you're not ready to go back to Crucible . . . Okay. Don't go. But I'm here, and I'm on your side. And I'm not going anywhere."

"I can't do this, Madison." Hudson's shoulders drop as his eyes close. "I can't."

He takes a step back and turns away from me. "How am I supposed to trust myself with you? Huh?" When he finally looks at me, an ocean of hurt fills his deep blue eyes.

"How am I supposed to touch you with the same hands . . ." His breathing grows ragged. "*How* can you want me to?"

My heart cracks wide open as tears pool behind my lids.

Desperate to fix this for him but knowing I can't. "Hudson . . ." I reach for his back, but he turns around.

His face is tight with an agony I wish he never had to know. "Why aren't you scared of me? You should be," he yells. "I'm a fucking monster, Madison. All my years of training, and I killed him." He yanks at his hair, tortured. "For a belt. For a fucking title. I killed a man. How can you sleep in the same bed with me?"

With a quiet, shaky voice, I counter his yelling, "Because I'm in love with you." I take his face in my hands and refuse to let him pull away. "Because no matter how much you don't want to hear it, this is not your fault. I know you. I know the man you are. I know your heart. And you can try to push me away all you want, but I didn't wait my entire life to find you, just to let you go when things get tough."

"Maddie," he chokes and wraps me in his arms, fighting back tears. "I'm so fucking sorry, and I don't know how to fix it."

"Oh, Hudson. It can't be fixed. It's not fair. It's awful. It's cruel. And there's no reason for any of it. But life's not fair. We both know that. And here's the thing. You're not alone. I'm here, and I'm not going anywhere." I breathe him in, refusing to let go. "Ever."

Hud pulls back with red eyes and hesitantly brushes his lips over mine.

I savor every second before I break the connection and take his hand. "Let's go do this, then we'll come back here to grab your bag and pack mine, okay?"

He nods silently, but doesn't push me away again, so I count it as a small victory.

HUDSON

By the time I walk into my bedroom, it's late. The sun set hours ago, and exhaustion has set in. Bone deep. Soul deep. Like I've trained for eighteen hours straight, but in reality, I spent most of the day quietly thinking about life.

My life. Mason's life. His wife and unborn baby's lives.

Trying to figure out the point in any of it, and how I'm supposed to go on like I didn't take a man's life. Like this isn't a pain I'll live with and feel every day for the rest of my life. It's senseless. And it's haunting me.

Jesus, I sound like a whiny little bitch.

Maddie is lying in bed, curled on her side. The sun set over the lake hours ago, and she's thrown on the black dress shirt I'd taken off earlier. The sleeves are rolled up, and the top few buttons are undone, giving me a glimpse of cleavage and miles of bare, toned legs. Her soft hair falls down around her shoulders, and her bottom lip is caught between her teeth while she reads something on her tablet.

"What are you doing, Mads?" I strip off my pants and climb into bed next to her, trying to catch a glimpse of the screen before she quickly closes the device.

"Reading Cooper's sister's newest book." She places the tablet on the nightstand, then runs her fingers through my hair as a pretty flush creeps up her skin.

It's funny . . . our roles have reversed.

She touches me so freely now, and I'm the one who wants to flinch away. I can't help but want to avoid tainting her with the blood permanently covering my hands. But I'm not willing to give her up either. A stronger man probably could have. A better man, maybe. But I'm stronger and better when I'm with her. "You told me you loved me earlier," I whisper.

Her fingers still, and piercing blue eyes hold mine hostage. "I know what I said, and I meant it."

"I didn't say it back." I cup her delicate face in my hands, pushing past the anxiety at the sight of my hands on her perfect skin. "But I do, you know."

Her hands cover mine, and she turns her face to press her lips to my palms.

"I love you so damn much, it scares me, baby. Because I don't know if I'm a good enough man to keep you."

Maddie sits up quickly and straddles my lap. The pretty flush from moments ago has been replaced with fierce determination. "Were you a good enough man two weeks ago?"

I drag my eyes up her body. "I thought I was."

She presses her lips to mine, breathing me in.

Taking my breath away and giving me life.

"Nothing has changed, Hudson. You're the same man today that you were the day I met you. What happened was a horrible accident. It could have happened during any fight. No one knew he had that condition. No. One. Not even Mason, or he wouldn't have been in that cage."

I trace my thumb along her jaw.

My hand shakes with the effort of holding back.

Needing to touch her, even though I should be pushing her away.

"You're alive, Hudson. You're here with me." Her lips brush over mine. As if reading my mind, she pushes against my chest. "I need you. Don't push me away."

My hands slide under her shirt and up her sides, stopping at the top of her rib cage. I run my thumb over her dragonfly, over her symbol of transformation and self-realization. This strong woman being forced to deal with another shit hand in life. "You're too good for me, Maddie."

I cup both of her breasts in my hands, and her responding moan has my cock aching and leaking in my boxers.

"You're mine, Hudson Kingston," she whispers against my lips, soft and sweet and setting me on edge. "And I'm not letting go."

The electricity crackles between us.

Demanding more.

No longer tender.

Hunger fueling us both.

"I'm yours, baby, and I fucking need you." I rip my lips from hers and drag them down her delicate throat, sucking the soft spot where her neck meets her shoulders. I graze my teeth over that spot until the heat of her pussy grinding down against my cock threatens to drive us both insane.

Maddie tilts her head, giving me better access. Then she yanks on my hair, pulls my head back roughly, and bites my lip. "Then take me."

I shuck off my boxers and push the scrap of lace covering her pussy aside. My fingers trace the lips of her wet pussy, then slide inside her sex. First one, then a second, all while my cock throbs beneath her. Aching and desperate and wanting.

"You're so wet for me, Maddie." She rides my fingers while the heel of my palm presses against her swollen clit. I run my lips along her throat. "You want me to fuck you, baby?"

She whimpers and grinds down, wanting more from me. Needing it. And when I take my hand away, she cries out until I press the head of my cock against her core and thrust into her warm body until I bottom out. Until there's no room between us. Until we're one, and we moan in unison.

"Hudson . . ." she keens and rips the starched shirt over her head.

Her tight pink nipples are two hard little peaks on her full breasts. High and firm and goddamned perfect when I suck them into my mouth and fuck into my girl.

I wrap an arm around her and grab her ass, kneading the delicate skin. My finger slips between her cheeks and dances down the crack of her ass. I push further until I get to where we're joined and run it through the juices already dripping between us, then slide back up until I'm circling that forbidden hole.

She gasps and hums as the walls of her pussy flutter around me with just the tiniest push of my index finger in sync with my cock.

Maddie moans with short little breaths, each higher pitched than the last as she buries her head in my neck and pushes against me until I'm knuckle-deep and fucking both her holes.

"That's it, baby. You like it when I fill you up? The way my cock fucks your pretty pussy while my finger fills your virgin ass?"

A strangled mess of sounds and words falls from her lips

as her already impossibly hot, tight cunt clamps down harder, choking my dick. "Oh, God." She throws her head back and closes her eyes.

"Eyes on me, Madison." I slow my strokes, prolonging her orgasm. "I'm the one making you come. The only one who ever fucking will, and you're watching me do it."

Once she goes limp in my arms, I flip us over without ever losing our connection, and her body comes alive again.

I pull out slowly and slam back into her, watching her back arch and her perfect tits bounce with each thrust.

She brings her knees up and cradles me between her thighs, meeting me thrust for thrust, grabbing my hips, digging her nails into the flesh of my ass. A possessiveness is in her eyes I recognize, mirroring my own.

I take both her hands in mine and slide my body over hers until we're chest to chest. Sweaty and slick. My cock throbs inside her, the base grinding against her clit. Holding both hands above her head, flat to the mattress, I set a slow, almost lazy pace.

It's practically burning me from the inside out to keep myself from fucking her like a wild animal. To take what I want and show her how good mindless fucking can be. But I'm not ready for this to be over. Not yet. Not ever.

She bucks against me, trying to top from the bottom, and I laugh.

"Oh, sunshine." I pull my hips back, then move both her wrists into one of my hands, so I can use the other to tease her clit with the head of my cock.

Maddie moans and writhes against me as I slide the tip in, then out again. Changing the tempo. The angle. Teasing her. Giving her enough to have her wanting. Needy and begging.

She whimpers and whines. "Hud. Oh my God. Hudson . . ." She drags my name out as I push in further this time.

Prolonging this.

Needing everything about it.

Needing my connection to her—to us—to last forever.

She tugs against the grip I have on her wrists, desperately trying to force me to give her what she wants. Again. And I smile a wicked smile.

"I know what this pussy needs." I finally let go of her wrists, and both my hands pin down her waist, holding her to the bed as I slam in and out of her, rolling my hips and rubbing against her walls over and over again.

"Hudson," she chants. "Hudson. *Hudson.*"

I take her lips in a blistering kiss as my orgasm wraps itself around the base of my spine, pushing against the confines of my body before finally splintering and filling her.

Maddie's body milks every last drop from me.

Our lips still tangled.

Her hands run up and down my back as her legs twine around my waist.

"I love you," she whispers.

"You own my heart, sunshine."

HUDSON

Friday morning, I leave Maddie sleeping in my bed and go for a run around the lake to clear my head. The cold air of November has turned frigid as we come closer to mid-December. But it feels good to be outside. The houses along the lake are just waking up as I lap around the frozen falls, pushing my muscles until they burn. I'm alone with my thoughts, trying to reconcile what everyone has been saying with what I know deep in my gut.

Mason McGuire is dead because he stepped into that ring with me.

Did he have a preexisting condition he was unaware of?

Yes.

But did I strike the blow that ended his life and took him away from his wife and child?

I did.

Can I ever step foot in that cage again, knowing that?

I'm not sure.

My thoughts are plagued with doubt during the entire five miles around the lake. It's only after I've stretched and walk back into my kitchen that my mind clears and calms.

My two favorite women sit at my kitchen table.

Not that I'd ever tell my sisters that.

Imogen and Maddie are sharing a plate of scrambled eggs when they both look up.

"I guess we need a grocery delivery if you've got to share breakfast, ladies." I drop a kiss on Maddie's head and grab a bottle of water from the fridge. "Hey, Gen. What's up?"

"What's up?" she repeats and chokes back her laugh.

"I'm just going to leave you two to talk." Maddie stands and runs her hand over my arm, and that simple touch soothes me. "There's an omelet on the stove for you." She presses her lips quickly to mine, and Imogen makes a gagging noise before Maddie leaves the room.

"Get your omelet and sit, Kingston. I'm done tiptoeing around." She scoops eggs onto her toast, folds it in half, and eats it like a sandwich, which is something she's done for years.

I grab my breakfast and smile at the thought of Maddie making it for me, even though it's not a pretty omelet. Once I'm seated across from Imogen, I take a bite of my lukewarm eggs, knowing her eyes are on me.

"Is Maddie being here a good sign?" she questions.

"A good sign of what?" I know I'm being thickheaded, but I'm not exactly sure what she's asking.

She rolls her eyes and brings a napkin to her mouth. "Well, let's see. A good sign that you're talking. A good sign that you haven't cut *everyone* in your life *out* of your life. A good sign that you haven't completely given up on living your life because of what happened." She balls the napkin in her hands and throws it at my face. "I've been fucking worried about you, you jerk. And you've been ignoring my calls. You're ignoring Cade's calls. Scarlet says you're ignoring everyone. So, I'm thinking Maddie is our only hope to get you through this."

"Imogen—"

"Don't you dare *Imogen* me. I've been your best friend for ten years. And you shut me out," she yells.

"I've shut everyone out," I counter, only I'm much calmer. "I don't know what I'm doing, Gen. I'm not you. I don't need to talk about everything right away. I need to process it before I can talk. I'm trying. But I'm working on it."

"Since when?" she pushes.

I consider my answer carefully. "Since last night."

"Why? What happened last night?"

She never did know when to drop it. "Since I realized I had something bigger than myself . . . Something more important than just me to fight for."

I'm expecting her to give me shit for that person being Maddie and not her or my family, but she doesn't. And I'm an asshole for even thinking that. That's not Imogen, and it never *has* been. Not with me.

"Remind me to thank Maddie then." She reaches across my plate and steals a big chunk of egg, red pepper, and cheese, then snags a piece of my toast.

"For what? Breakfast?" I push the rest of my plate in front of her.

"No. I love Mads, but she's not exactly a good cook. It's pretty hard to mess up eggs . . . I mean, it's edible, but"—she shakes her head—"whatever. I meant you, you big baboon. For getting through to you on a level the rest of us couldn't."

She makes another egg sandwich but leaves it sitting on her plate. "I've known you a long time, Hud. I was there when Lenny and Jace's mom died and then a few years later when your dad died. I was there when you found out about Amelia and when you wanted to kill my brother for sleeping with your sister. I've been there for everything since we were sixteen years old, and I've never not been able to get through to you before. But she did. She's really good for you, Hud. Don't let her go."

"I'm not letting her go. Ever." As the words leave my mouth, my resolve strengthens.

I know, without a shadow of a doubt, Madison Dixon was always meant to be mine.

"Then you need to start living again. Because right now, you're hiding. And that's not the Hudson Kingston I know."

She reaches across the table and squeezes my hand, then pushes my plate back toward me. "Now eat up and get back to the gym before you get flabby and she dumps you."

I rest my hand on top of hers. "Thanks, Gen."

"Anytime."

My conversation with Imogen plays on repeat in my mind for the rest of the day. I've always been a man of action. Until this past week.

It's like I've been paralyzed with guilt and remorse.

With self-doubt and self-loathing.

But Maddie has a way of getting under my skin that no one else ever has.

The sun is already setting that afternoon when I step into the living room. Maddie sits on the couch in front of the fireplace, the flames lighting her pretty face, and a cup of tea in her hand. She has her open MacBook on her lap and a notebook on the table in front of her. Her hair is piled on top of her head in a messy bun with a pen sticking out of it.

She's messy and stunning.

And when she hears me, and lifts her eyes to mine, her smile is everything.

I swear to God, my heart skips a beat, and I have to remind myself to breathe.

"What'cha working on, baby?" I sit down next to her and pull her legs across my lap.

With a sigh, she closes her computer and moves it to the side. "The social-media campaign for Start A Revolution's holiday food drive. It ends next week. I promised Daphne one more big push before then."

I dig my fingers into the arch of her foot, and she moans. "Ohh. That feels nice."

"Move in with me," I blurt the words out with absolutely no couth whatsoever.

Maddie startles. "*What*? Are you serious?"

"Yeah, I am. Move in with me, Madison. Having you here feels right. This is where you're supposed to be." With each word I say, another piece of our puzzle clicks into place, completing the picture of the life I want. The one she deserves even if I don't. "I want you to be the first person I see in the morning, and I want to be the last one you see at night."

"Hudson . . . we've barely been together for a week." She runs her teeth over her bottom lip nervously. "It's so *fast*." The last word comes out more like a question than an answer.

"We've known each other for three years, sunshine." I drop her feet and pull her into my lap. "And I know I love you. I know that's not changing."

"Hud . . ." She closes her eyes and leans her head against my chest before looking back up. "This is crazy. I feel like I'm about to jump off a cliff."

"Take my hand. Let's jump together."

She thinks about it for a long minute before her dimples pop deep in her cheeks as she nods her head.

"Is that a yes, Mads?" I ask, hope blooming in my chest. "I need to hear the words."

"You're crazy, Hudson. You know that, right?"

I shrug, and she runs her fingers through my hair. "I'm not sure I was planning on leaving anyway."

"Thanks for fighting for me, baby."

With her eyes open and fixed on me, she brushes her lips over mine and hums deep in her throat. "Never underestimate a woman in love, Hudson Kingston. I waited my whole life to feel this. To feel you. And I refuse to let anything tear us apart."

"I'm not sure what I did to deserve you, sunshine." My smile stretches clear across my face for the first time in what feels like a long damn time.

"It's you, Hudson. You didn't have to do anything but be you." I hold her face in my hands and press my lips to her forehead. I kiss her nose and cheeks, her long lashes and soft dimples before taking her mouth in a kiss hot enough to scorch the sun.

My phone rings in my pocket, but I ignore it.

Not wanting to break this moment.

It stops, then immediately starts ringing again.

Maddie groans and shoves her hand in my pants to pull it out.

"A little to the left," I tell her jokingly before she elbows me in the side.

"I'm getting your phone, Hud. It's smaller and has less metal in it than your dick."

I laugh. "Not exactly a solid burn, Mads."

She hands me the phone, and we look at Hunter's name flashing across the screen.

"Take the call, Hud." She scoots off my lap and tucks her knees under herself while I run my finger across the screen and answer.

"Hey, Hunt. Did you get it?"

Maddie looks at me questioningly.

"Yeah, man. I got it. Are you sure about this?" I asked

Hunter to get me Leona McGuire's phone number and address. I need to see her. I need to talk to her. To let her rage and blame me, if that's what she needs. I owe her that much.

Leona agreed to see me on Sunday morning.

Maddie wanted to come with me—hell, my entire family wanted to come with me. But this is something I need to do for myself. For Mason. Only now, as I'm sitting in front of their house, I'm not sure I can get out of the car, and I'm wishing I'd taken one of them up on their offer.

I grab my phone and hit Sawyer's number on my speed dial while I take in the modest ranch-style house. The blue wooden siding and cracked sidewalks show the home's age, but it's been well-kept. Frozen flower beds line either side of the front door. White twinkling Christmas lights hang from the roof. And a big picture window, covered by sheer white curtains, looks out over the street I'm parked on.

Sawyer answers after two rings. "Hey, man. You there already?"

"Yeah. Got here a few minutes ago. What are you doing?" I take a deep breath and watch the drizzle of icy rain bounce against my windshield.

"Well, it's ten o'clock on a Sunday morning. I worked until three a.m. So I'm still in bed, asshole." His words are sarcastic, but there's no heat in his voice.

"Sorry." The white curtains shift, and I realize my time is running out. "Tell me I need to do this. That I'm not being a selfish prick. That I'm giving her closure as much as I'm trying to get some for myself."

"You're not a selfish dick, Hudson. Tell her what you need to say and be prepared to take anything she throws your way without defending yourself at all. Give her the chance to hate you. And know we're all here in your corner."

"Thanks, brother." I end the call and stare out the windshield for another long moment before finally growing a set of balls and jogging to the front door.

I raise my hand to knock, but it opens before I get a chance, and a kid half my size stands on the other side. He's got dark eyes and dark hair like Mason did. He looks like he's ten years old, tops. "Wasn't sure if you were going to chicken out."

"Neither was I." I look around the room for Leona but come up empty. "Is Leona home?"

"Yeah. She'll be out in a minute. She doesn't like you very much," he says with the brutal honesty only a kid has.

"To be fair, I don't know if I like me very much either."

"Daniel." Leona steps into the living room and glares at the kid. "Would you give us a minute?"

"Sure, Mom." He walks by Leona, and she runs a hand over his curly black hair as he goes.

"Mom?" I ask. They never mentioned Mason and Leona already having a kid.

She must recognize my unspoken question. "He isn't biologically mine, but he's mine in every way that matters." She rubs her pregnant belly, then sits on the couch. "Why are you here, King?"

I run my hands over my face.

Jesus, this is hard.

"I'm not exactly sure. I guess I wanted to give you a chance to hate me in person. I thought maybe it would help you to be able—" I cut myself off midsentence. "I don't know what I thought. But I guess I was hoping you'd let me tell you how sorry I am. I never meant—"

"To kill him?" she cuts me off, then laughs. "If it wasn't you, it would have been the next opponent or the one after that. The doctor told me he was a walking time bomb. He just didn't know it. It didn't even have to happen in that damn cage."

She wipes her eyes. "He was so excited to get to fight you. So proud of what he'd earned. Seems kind of fitting in a really fucked up way."

"I wish . . ." I swallow, trying to keep my quickly disintegrating composure. "God, I'm just so fucking sorry."

"You couldn't have known. We didn't even know." A tear slips down her cheek, and my gut clenches. "He loved what he did, King. He loved it every single day. And he was a man who lived every single day full-out. No regrets. We can't turn back the clock, no matter how much I wish we could. Life doesn't work that way."

"Do you need anything?" I ask, not sure what I could do for her.

"You can't give me back what I need." Her voice trembles. "But you can do something for me."

"Name it."

"Keep fighting. Mason would be so mad if he knew you stopped fighting. He followed your career for years. Hometown Philly guy fighting all over the world. Winning belts everywhere you went. The highlight of his career was having the chance to fight you. And now, the reports are you're retiring."

"I haven't spoken to anyone about my plans yet. I haven't made any decisions." Retirement has crossed my mind every day since I heard the news, but I'd only shared that with Maddie and Cade.

"I don't hate you, King. I hate the sport he loved. I hate the fates that took him from us. I hate you for winning because I wish he'd gotten that belt. But I don't hate you. I don't even know you." She stands from the couch and walks to the door. "Don't feel bad for me. I lived more every day that Mason loved me than most people do in a lifetime."

I join her at the door. "Thank you for letting me stop by today, Leona. If you ever need anything, you've got my number."

She nods and opens the door.

And as I slide behind the wheel of my car, my shoulders feel lighter than they have in a while.

I wasn't expecting anything from Leona McGuire.

But what she just gave me was everything.

MADDIE

*C*ade let me cancel my classes last week, but after Hudson and I discussed it when he got home last night, we decided we'd both go back to the gym on Monday. For him, that was this morning. For me, it's tonight, and it feels good to be back. This is my last week of classes until January. Cade always suspends classes during the holidays.

Usually, I get antsy, thinking about two weeks of not teaching.

I don't just love teaching yoga for the extra paycheck and sense of security it helps me maintain. I love it for the way it clears my mind and strengthens my soul. Teaching even helps center me. I'm more focused after a class. More relaxed. Those two weeks without my classes, and what they do for me, suck. But not this year.

This year, I'm thinking about Hudson's sunroom and how much I'm looking forward to bringing my mat in there in the mornings. I'm thinking about long, late nights in bed with him and lazy mornings together. Christmas has never been high on my list of priorities. Brandon and I never made a big deal out of it before, and it's never bothered me. But I think this year will be different.

It'll be the first year I make new traditions.

"What's got you smiling like that, sunshine?" Hudson asks as I clean my last mat of the night.

"Nothing," I tell him coyly, checking quickly to see who's around and am pleasantly surprised to find the gym completely empty. "Well, nothing I want to talk about here." I lift up on my toes and kiss his lips, savoring the taste of him.

"You almost ready?" His hand slips to my lower back, resting on the bare skin just above my yoga pants, and my blood heats under his touch.

I nod, unable to speak, and the cocky grin stretching across his face holds delicious promises.

"Get a room," Cade yells with a laugh.

"Sorry." I blush, mortified.

"Ignore him, Mads. He's just mad he can't tell me *no girls* anymore." Hudson puffs up his chest like a proud peacock before I smack his pec.

"I'm a woman, not a girl. And I better be the only one." I smile sweetly but with a little threat.

Cade smacks Hud's back. "She told you."

"Whatever. Like my sister doesn't keep your balls in her Chanel bag," Hudson chuckles.

With a devious glint in his eyes, Cade smirks. "Oh, your sister can do anything she wants with my balls. I have no complaints."

"Jesus Christ, man. Gross. *Fuck.* What the hell?" Hud pinches his lips together, and Cade and I crack up.

"Oh my God. You two are ridiculous." I put away the cleaning solution and grab my bag from the locker room. "I'm ready."

Cade shuts off the lights, and the three of us walk out

together, expecting an empty parking lot, not the ambush we walk into.

As soon as we step out of the building, a camera is shoved in our faces. A reporter stands next to the camera man. And Spider Reynolds, the creep Hudson almost fought at Kingdom weeks ago, is with them, surrounded by a bunch of his team.

"What the hell is going on here?" Cade demands, vibrating with anger.

"Go inside, Madison." Hudson steps in front of me with Cade sliding next to him to block me from these men.

"Yeah, that's right. You wouldn't want your woman to see what a pussy you really are, King."

I don't move.

"This is private property, and I want you off it now before I call the cops," Cade threatens. But Reynolds continues eyeing up Hudson.

"I bet you feel like a tough guy now, huh, King. You think you're a killer." I fist the back of Hudson's hoodie and look around him as Spider continues, "That you're untouchable. You still too fucking scared to fight me? Or did your balls finally drop after killing a worthless fighter like McGuire?"

Hudson's body is rigid as Reynolds gets in his face.

"You know, when your girl wants to fuck a real man, she imagines it's *me* fucking her, King. I can get the job done in all the ways you never will." He pushes Hudson's chest, and I try to sidestep Hud to see what else is going on, but he and Cade move closer together.

"He's twice the fighter you'll ever be, Reynolds. Now, you've said your peace. Get the fuck off my property," Cade threatens.

"If your boy is twice the fighter I am, then he'll fight me like a man instead of hiding behind his family's money and his coach's name."

"You wanna talk big. You want this fight because you say you wanna prove you're better than me? That I'm just a name with a trust fund? Just wanna prove something, right? And this isn't about the money, is it? It's about showing the world that I'm a joke." Hudson takes a step forward, and I drop my hold on him. "Fine. You name the time and the place, and I'll fight you."

Reynolds smiles, thinking he's won, but I can tell from Hudson's stance, something else is going on here.

"I'll fight you on one condition."

Reynolds posturing stops, and he glares. "Pussy boy needs a condition," he announces to his buddies and the reporter. "They won't even call you *Prince* after I'm done with you, Kingston. You'll be a fucking joker in my court."

"So, you agree to my condition then?" There's a cockiness to Hudson's voice I recognize, but Reynold's isn't picking up on it. I don't know what Hud's up to. Though I can tell it's something good.

"One condition, and you'll fight me for your belt?" Reynolds turns to the camera. "You're getting this on tape, right? I don't want this soft-fight, pansy-ass motherfucker to be able to back out."

The camera man nods, and Reynolds turns back to Hudson. "Name the condition."

"Agree to it now, and I'll fight you for my belt as soon as they can set it up," Hud pushes.

Reynolds finally eyes Hudson carefully before agreeing. "Now, what the fuck do you want?"

"We donate every penny either of us earns from the fight to Mason McGuire's wife. No questions asked. No exceptions. She gets both payouts. Mine and yours. Agree, and this will be the only shot you ever get at my belt."

I look between Hudson and Reynolds, watching these two intimidating men dancing this intricate dance, and fear slivers down my spine. There's a dangerous charge in the cold air, making every hair on my body stand on edge.

Reynolds stares at Hudson in disbelief. "No fucking way," he shouts.

"No sweat off my back. I can live my life with the belt I've earned five times. You're the dick who turned down your chance."

The standoff between the two of them grows impossibly tense until Cade takes a step forward. "He's made his decision, King. Let's go."

"I'll do it," Reynolds growls low, and a murmur of voices erupts from the group of men surrounding him, but he silences them with a look. "I want it soon, King. Deal's off if you need months to get this done."

Hudson scoffs like that's the most ridiculous thing he's ever heard. "I'll call my agent. I could fight you tomorrow and win, asshole."

"Now walk away," Cade tells them as he holds his hands up in front of the camera. Then he pulls his phone from his pocket and makes a call.

Hudson holds his hand out to me behind his back, and I grasp on to it while I continue to peek around him wordlessly. He doesn't move until they're out of the parking lot, then he finally spins around. "I told you to go inside."

I step into him and wrap my hands around his waist. "I didn't say anything this time, and I didn't get in the way." I lay my head against his chest. "Are you really going to fight him?"

Cade hangs up and joins us.

"He'll never leave me alone if I don't." His fingers run through my hair, and I shiver.

"Can you win?"

Cade and Hudson look at each other and laugh.

I guess that's a good sign.

The rest of the week passes by without another incident. The fight is scheduled for the second week in January. Hudson swears he'll be fine. But it makes me worry, even if he says I don't need to.

Right now, I'm trying desperately not to focus on the way my stomach churns every time I think about him stepping into the cage again. Meanwhile, he's hyperfocusing on a Christmas tree. He had an errand to run earlier today but made me promise I'd come with him to pick out a tree this afternoon.

"What about this one?" Hudson stands next to a towering evergreen in the middle of what's touted as Kroydon Hill's oldest Christmas tree farm. "How tall is this thing?"

Jace groans next to me. "Too fucking tall. What the hell, Hud?"

"Your debt's not paid until you help me get it into the house and decorated, jackoff." He holds the measuring stick up next to the tree, and the tree towers over the ten-foot-tall stick. "I think this is the one." His goofy grin grows. "Do you like it, sunshine?"

I giggle. "Hudson, I've literally had tiny Charlie Brown trees my whole life. I've slept in houses whose roofs weren't that tall. Get whatever you want."

"Give it up, Maddie. Hud loves Christmas," Jace warns me.

And that's how I end up spending the next hour watching these two fight over how to strap a monstrously large tree to Hudson's truck. Them trying to get it into the house was even funnier. Especially when Cooper came over to help. Carys and I popped a bag of popcorn and laughed while the three of them argued their way through standing it up in the center of the family room.

It only fell over twice. *Twice*. A twelve-foot tree fell over *twice*, and miraculously managed to miss every piece of furniture and every human in the room. I haven't laughed this hard in years. Eventually Sawyer stopped by. He didn't tell Hudson Jace called him in as backup, but he did tell me, then swore me to secrecy.

I wouldn't necessarily call him helpful though.

There may have been a chainsaw brought inside the house at one point.

Yup. *Inside the house.* They decided the trunk was crooked.

I didn't have the heart to tell him we should have gotten the Charlie Brown tree I wanted. Carys and I sat there the entire time with tears streaming down our faces from laughing so hard.

Eventually, the tree stood on its own, albeit a little crooked. But there was no way I was telling them that. Chloe brought pizza, and our ragtag group ate, laughed, and did the worst job I've ever seen decorating a tree. But it was more fun than I remember having in years.

And now that everyone has left, and it's well past midnight, Hudson drags me back into the living room to stand under the mistletoe and caresses my cheek. "I love you, Maddie."

"I love you too, Hud." I run my hands up his arms, and he winces. "What's wrong?"

Hudson reaches back and pulls his dark thermal shirt over his head. His bicep is wrapped in plastic wrap. "Did you get a new tattoo today? Was that your errand?"

He ignores my questions and peels back the wrapping, then flexes.

On his bicep is my dragonfly flying in front of the sun. It blends perfectly into his sleeve, like it was always supposed to be there. "Hudson," I gasp and ghost my finger around it without touching. "It's beautiful."

"Do you like it?" He looks nervous, like a little boy who spent all his allowance on a present and is afraid the recipient will be disappointed.

"The detail is amazing. The watercolor purples and greens. They're perfect." Suddenly, tears sting the back of my eyes. "I can't believe you inked me on your skin."

"I wanted us to make the next big change in our lives together, Maddie. And I wanted something to symbolize that. Every line on my skin tells a story." He runs a hand over the script on his chest. "I got *Only the good die young* when my stepmother died." Then he flexes his bicep and tells me each story behind the ink on his body. Until he finally holds up his hand.

"There's nothing there. You don't have anything on your hands, Hud."

"No. Not yet, baby. I'm not really a ring guy, So I thought once we're married, I could get one tatted on my finger." Hud tries to drop to his knee, but I quickly grab his arm, stopping him, and my stomach somersaults.

"Hudson . . . please don't. Not yet." He looks at me with hurt in his dark-blue eyes. "Hud. You're so sure of the world and your place in it that you jump and know everything will be fine. That's not me. I need to move a little slower than that."

"But you agreed to move in. I love you, Maddie. And I know you love me." He holds my hand gently in his, and for a second, I kick myself for stopping what, no doubt, would have been a beautiful proposal.

My entire body trembles as butterflies take flight in my stomach. "I do love you with my whole soul. I just don't handle change well. I'm a little slower than you. I'm not saying I don't want to marry you. I'm just saying I need to process these past few weeks a little longer before I'm ready to think about what comes next."

He picks me up, and I wrap my legs around his waist. "Fine," he pouts. "But I know what I want, Mads. And I'm not good at waiting. Any idea how long it'll be until I get my prize?"

"I've never been anyone's prize before." There go those butterflies again.

"I keep telling you, Maddie. You're my everything."

When he kisses me, I think I finally believe him.

HUDSON

"Merry Christmas, baby."

The smile gracing Maddie's beautiful face is magnificent. She's been swaying with Serena in her arms for a while now, while my family gathers in Max and Daphne's living room, exchanging presents. When I step up behind her and wrap my arms around her middle, she leans back against me, never tearing her eyes off Serena.

"Isn't she the most perfect thing you've ever seen?" The awe in her voice shouldn't make me hard, but basically *everything* Maddie does makes me hard.

A fact she notices quickly as I press against her ass.

"Hudson." She glares over her shoulder, never breaking the rhythm of her sway.

Max moves next to the tree and holds up a champagne flute. "I'd like to make a toast."

A few of us groan because my oldest brother tends to be a little long-winded when it comes to toasts. But the deliriously happy look that's been plastered on his face since Serena was born doesn't budge an inch. Daphne and Serena have definitely mellowed Maximus out.

Daphne carefully takes Serena from Maddie, and I slide my arm up and wrap it across Maddie's chest, holding her close enough to rest my chin on top of her head.

My nieces, nephews, and little sister all sit in a towering mess of ripped wrapping paper and empty boxes. Some play with their new toys. Others are more interested in the boxes. Maddie can't take her eyes off them.

And while Max drones on about the meaning of family and how lucky we all are to have ours, I can't help but feel dazzled by this woman in my arms. "You want one of them one day, Mads?"

"One of what?" she whispers back.

I angle her toward all six kids. "A posse of Kingstons?"

"The only way we're having six kids is if *you're* pushing them out of your body. No way I'm doing that six times."

Max glares at us as he raises his glass high in the air and finishes his toast. "To family. Merry Christmas."

Merry Christmas echoes throughout the room, and I spin Maddie in my arms to face me.

"How many do you think you want?" The idea of her pregnant with my baby lights a whole new fire inside me.

"How about we start with one and go from there, King." She licks her lips, and my cock pulses between us.

"You gotta marry me first, Mads." I'm gonna wear her down sooner or later.

Scarlet walks by and smacks the back of my head. "Leave her alone, you hornball." She grabs Maddie's hand and drags her out of the room. "Come with me, Maddie. Let's get you a real drink so I can smell the liquor. I've got seven more months of this before I can have another drink, and my little brother is already trying to get you to agree to it." She rolls her eyes, and I hear her muttering to Maddie about traveling and getting as many miles out of her bikinis as she can before she agrees to get pregnant and give her body over to a demon spawn.

Maddie turns her head back to me and mouths *help*, just as I'm handed a shot of the 150-year-old bourbon Sawyer brought, and the conversations grow more nostalgic. Remembering all the old Christmases we had before Dad died, and all the traditions we still try to carry on today.

Max is right.

Family is everything.

And that woman in the other room is every bit as much my family as my brothers and sisters are. With or without my ring on her finger, she's it.

THE NEXT MORNING, the alarm goes off at the crack of dawn, and I hit snooze.

Guess there's a first time for everything because I never hit snooze. Snooze is for quitters. It's for procrastinators. It's not for champions. At least, that's what I used to think. But that was before I was waking up with a boner and a beautiful woman who's naked in my bed.

I lay there, staring at the ceiling, trying to convince myself to move.

It's not working.

I want to slide inside her hot body.

I want to taste her pussy on my lips.

I want to feel her walls clamping down on me.

I want to spend the week fucking her—morning, noon, and night. But we can't always get what we want. And while Cade can't tell me *no women* anymore, he can absolutely tell me *no sex*. It's only two weeks. I can do this. I've gone without longer than two weeks before, but that was before Maddie.

Before sex became a religious experience. And sweet baby Jesus in the manger, I'll be damned if I don't see God when I sink inside her body.

When the alarm goes off again, she drapes her arm over my chest before trying to pull me closer, but I stay stiff. *Stay stiff.* Ha ha ha.

"I've got to get up, Mads." I press my lips to her spine and groan when she rolls over.

Her perfect tits are begging for attention.

"You're making this hard, Mads." *Making this hard.* I laugh silently again. I've definitely got sex on the brain.

She half moans and half snores. "Just a quickie, Hud. It's the best way to start the day." One eye opens and looks at me through the blonde hair covering her face.

"No can do, sunshine. You know the rules. No sex until after the fight," I tease her.

She groans as her hand traces a path over my abs before I stop her.

"No can do, babe." And idea comes to me, and I figure *why the hell not?* "Cade said since you're not my wife, no sex until the fight. But if we were married . . ." I leave the rest of the lie hanging in the air.

Okay. I can cross that attempt off as a mistake when she literally kicks my ass out of bed.

Actually kicks me with her foot.

"Be careful at the gym. I'll see you tonight." She rolls away and snuggles back under the covers while I stand up and smile.

I'm wearing her down.

HUDSON

I keep asking Maddie to marry me.

JACE

Why?

HUDSON

Why what?

JACE

Why do you keep asking? Did she say no?

HUDSON

. . .

BECKET

OMFG. She said no?!?

JACE

Dude. Stop. You're telling me you asked her once and she said no. And you asked again?

HUDSON

She loves me. She just thought we were moving too fast.

MAX

Then try listening to her, shithead, and slow your roll.

SAWYER

Swear to God, Maxipad. You talk like you're eighty, not forty.

MAX

I'm not forty, shithead.

BECKET

Then stop talking like it.

MAX

What forty-year-old says slow your roll?

HUDSON

Hello . . . Assholes . . . Anybody got any actual advice?

SAWYER

Try listening to her, Hud. Enjoy where you are now and don't rush it. She'll let you know when she's ready.

JACE

In the meantime, I have one word . . . yoga sex.

BECKET

That's two words, jackoff.

SAWYER

It's a good thing you're pretty, kid.

IN A LOT OF WAYS, the next two weeks fly by.

It wasn't like my body took a beating in my fight against Mason McGuire, but my mind sure as hell did. So, Cade switched up my training for this fight. We still did the normal things, but he had me do yoga with Maddie for an hour every day.

He wanted me to find my zen. He thought it would help center me.

I guess it did. Once I got into meditating, I could see the draw of it.

The only problem is I'm supposed to be clearing my mind, and every time she wears her tight little booty shorts and sports bras, then leans over my body to adjust my posture, my zen goes flying out the fucking window while all the blood working to keep it where it's supposed to be rushes to my cock.

Even now. Maddie and I are in the warm-up room in Las Vegas, waiting for them to give us the ten-minute warning so she has time to get to her seat before the fight, and she's working me through my breathing. Definitely different. Not bad though. I kinda wish I'd thought to do this for my earlier fights.

There's a knock on the door before Cade pops his head in. "Ten minutes, King. Sawyer is out here waiting to walk Maddie to her seat."

I nod, and he gives us a minute alone.

She stands in front of me in her tight black dress, sky-high heels lacing up her ankles, and her hair, that I fucking love, in fat curls around her shoulders. She's my every wet dream come to life, and I can't wait to win this fight so I can go back to our hotel room and fuck her brains out.

"You gonna be my prize again tonight, Mads?" I wrap a curl around my finger and smile.

"I'll do you one better, Kingston. You win this fight, and I'll marry you . . . tonight." She cocks one brow in challenge.

My heartbeat picks up speed. "What?"

"We're all here. Well, most of your siblings. My brother. Carys and Chloe. Win the fight, and we'll find an Elvis to marry us."

"In one of those white suits with the sparkles?" I joke because she can't be serious. "Don't joke with me, Maddie. Because I'm *going* to win this fight."

She takes a step back. "I know."

"Why now? What's changed?" I need to know.

"Marriage is a piece of paper to me, Hudson. But you . . . you're everything, and it matters to you. So, win the damn fight, and let's get married."

CHAMPIONSHIP FIGHTS ARE FIVE ROUNDS, five minutes each.

I took my own five minutes after Maddie left to get my head in the fight, as Cade likes to say. Visualizing the fight.

Pumping myself up. Preparing myself to step back into that cage. Knowing that I want to win, but I need the overall outcome to be different this time.

I need to destroy this fighter.

I need to dominate him.

But I need him to walk away.

When I walk through the door and join Cade, Cooper, and Jax as the first chords of Avenged Sevenfold plays over the roar of the crowd, I picture the takedown. I feel the ref holding my hand in the air. I will the fight into my submission.

I'm going to win.

Round 1

Spider comes out swinging as soon as the bell rings.

I've always said he projects every move before he makes it, and tonight's no different.

His frustration grows visible with each punch I dodge.

And when I smile after I block his kick with my knee, his confident facade cracks.

That's when I strike.

I hit him with a straight left jab to his nose and draw blood, knocking him off-balance.

"That all you got, King? I bet that girl of yours hits harder than that," he sneers, and I see red.

"She does hit harder than that, asshole. And she wouldn't be scared to knock your ass out, you piece of shit." I throw an uppercut, looking to knock him out cold and end this joke, but he dodges it with blood still dripping from his face.

"Shame I didn't get to taste her before you got in my way that night at Crucible. She's a pretty little thing, teaching that yoga class." His words catch me off guard, giving Spider the opportunity to land a kick in my ribs before realization dawns.

This mother fucker broke into the gym.

He's who went after Maddie.

And my vision blurs with a raging fury unlike anything I've ever felt before.

I go for a double-leg takedown.

Slam him to the ground.

Then from behind, I wrap my legs around his waist, and one arm slides down underneath his chin, squeezing off his oxygen. "You went after the wrong girl, cocksucker."

"It was supposed to be you," he wheezes while trying to break my hold.

But I got my answer and squeeze tighter until he starts to lose consciousness and taps my forearm. I ignore the tap, his beg for mercy, until I'm ripped away by the referee and declared the winner.

Once the announcement is over, Cade opens the door of the cage, and Maddie is the first to run in. I lift her high in the air, then bring her down and press my lips to hers. "Looks like I won, sunshine. You gonna give me my prize?"

"I'm gonna give you everything, King."

EPILOGUE

Maddie

"You sure this is what you want to do, Mads? Especially tonight?" Brandon has a nervous smile spread across his face as we wait for the night manager at the Graceland Wedding Chapel to tell us it's time. "I know Hud won, but he also sent Spider Reynolds to jail tonight."

"Did you see the Elvis we picked? He's old and fat and wearing a white-sequined jumpsuit. It's perfect, and I'm not letting anyone ruin it." I gently tap my flowers against his chest. "I don't care about Spider Reynolds. I don't care about the wedding itself, Brandon. I just care about Hudson. I don't need a piece of paper to tell me I'm in love. I just need him."

The balding manager turns to us as "Can't Help Falling In Love" starts to play over the sound system. "It's time."

When the doors open, all I see is Hudson.

Everything and everyone else disappears until I'm standing next to him.

Elvis walks us through our vows, and I ignore all his ridiculousness.

I stare into the dark-blue depths of Hudson's eyes and

pledge my life to him. To love him. Honor him. Trust him with my heart and soul and life. Then he pledges the same. I didn't think the words would matter to me. This man is already mine, and I know it in my bones. But something about tonight . . . about committing myself to him . . . it's perfect.

And when Hudson takes my face in his hands and kisses me as they announce us Mr. and Mrs. Hudson Kingston, a round of cheers rings out, reminding me just how many of our friends and family are here with us.

"I love you, Mr. Kingston." I wrap my arms around Hudson's neck and nuzzle my face against his.

Hud slides his hands down my body before he picks me up and carries me out of the chapel. "I love you, Mrs. Kingston. Forever."

"Always, Hud."

The End

AFTERWORD

Not ready to say goodbye to Hudson and Maddie yet?
Enjoy this free Bonus epilogue!
https://dl.bookfunnel.com/8l7mlff71b

Ready for the next books in The Defiant Kings Series?

Preorder Sawyer Kingston's story in Shaken: https://bit.ly/ShakenDefiantKings2

Preorder Jace Kingston's story in Iced: https://bit.ly/IcedDefiantKings3

AFTERWORD

Preorder Becket Kingston's story in Overruled: https://bit.ly/OverruledDefiantKings4

ACKNOWLEDGMENTS

Writing this book was the hardest experience of my life. I've been blessed with the kind of mother we all dream of having, and during the course of writing Hudson and Maddie's story, she was placed in hospice. I finished my final run through of this book sitting next to her bedside as I watched her take her final breaths.

I would not have made it through this process without the love and support of so many people.

Brianna and Heather ~ I will never be able to thank you enough for everything you have done for me. There are no words that feel big enough.

Dena ~ Without you, I would have never made this deadline and I will be forever grateful for your support, long voice memos and insane attention to detail.

Sarah ~ I will follow you anywhere.

Shannon ~ This cover is everything. Thank you for making Hudson perfect.

Vicki & Jen ~ I am so lucky to have you in my corner and to count you as my friends.

For all of my Jersey Girls ~ Thank you for giving me a safe space and showing me so much grace over the last few months.

To all of the Indie authors out there who have helped me along the way – you are amazing! This community is so incredibly supportive, and I am so lucky to be a part of it!

Thank you to all of the bloggers who took the time to read, review, and promote Caged. I promise to get the next book to you earlier!

And finally, the biggest thank you to you, the reader. I hope you enjoyed reading Hudson and Maddie as much as I loved being lost in their world.

ABOUT THE AUTHOR

Bella Matthews is a USA Today Bestselling Author. She's married to her very own Alpha Male and raising three little ones. You can typically find her running from one sporting event to another, or yelling from the sidelines. When she is home, she's usually hiding in her office with the only other female in the house, her rescue dog Tinker Bell by her side. She likes to write swoon-worthy heroes and sassy, smart, strong heroines with a healthy dose of laughter and all the feels. Big family dynamics are her favorite and sarcasm is her love language.

Stay Connected

Amazon Author Page: https://amzn.to/2UWU7Xs
Facebook Page: https://www.facebook.com/bella.matthews.3511
Reader Group: https://www.facebook.com/groups/599671387345008/
Instagram: https://www.instagram.com/bella.matthews.author/
Bookbub: https://www.bookbub.com/authors/bella-matthews
Goodreads: https://www.goodreads.com/.../show/20795160.Bella_Matthews
TikTok: https://vm.tiktok.com/ZMdfNfbQD/
Newsletter: https://bit.ly/BMNLsingups
Patreon: https://www.patreon.com/BellaMatthews

Printed in Great Britain
by Amazon